AFFAIR FOR THE BARON

Mario Ballas, a fabulously wealthy ex-criminal, lived in Mexico surrounded by art treasures and jewellery after the Baron's heart. The collection was protected by the old man's bodyguard of ruthless men, and when a valuable set of emerald pieces was stolen, the Baron was asked to investigate. He soon found that much more than art treasures were involved, and also found that the ex-gangster had ideals and dreams no one had suspected.

JOHN CREASEY
as
ANTHONY MORTON

AFFAIR FOR THE BARON

HODDER PAPERBACKS

COPYRIGHT © 1967 BY JOHN CREASEY
FIRST PUBLISHED BY HODDER AND STOUGHTON LTD 1967
HODDER PAPERBACK EDITION 1970

Printed in Great Britain for
Hodder Paperbacks Limited,
St. Paul's House, Warwick Lane, London, E.C.4,
by Cox and Wyman Ltd.,
London, Reading and Fakenham

ISBN 0 340 12794 5

CONTENTS

This book is dedicated to

Patsy and
Marshall Steves

whom I met by chance on board the S.S. *United States*; who made me so welcome at their unbelievably beautiful home in San Antonio, Texas; and who talked to me about *HemisFair*, then little more than a magnificent concept, with two years of tremendous effort lying ahead.

As Marshall Steves built *HemisFair*, I 'built' *Affair For The Baron* . . . and between us we built friendship, of which this book is a token.

CHAPTER ONE

Near Miss

THE girl nearly slipped as she jumped out of the yellow taxi, and the driver said :

"Careful, miss."

She gave a quick, almost haunted smile over her shoulder, and slammed the door, which did not latch. The taxi driver leaned over, struggling with the door as the girl ran towards the entrance of the station, carrying one small briefcase. Out of the corner of his eye, he saw a fallen glove; he heaved a great sigh, and bellowed :

"Hey, miss !"

Even if she heard, the girl ignored him.

The taxi driver watched her, still running, and was puzzled; no train was due to leave Pennsylvania Station in the next minute or so. He muttered : "What's the hurry?" Slowly descending from his taxi, he bumped into a young man jumping from a black sedan which was pulling up alongside. The man, short and lightly built, went staggering back; the taxi driver, solid as a piece of Brooklyn granite, glared irately.

What he saw startled him. There was sheer malevolence in the other's dark eyes; viciousness in the pale, handsome face. And behind him, the driver of the sedan was swearing.

The taxi driver, toughened and roughened by countless encounters with human nature, knew trouble when he saw it. He muttered again : "Excuse me," and rounded the back of his cab. The man he had bumped into recovered and raced off, and the sedan moved away. Looking over his shoulder, the taxi driver saw the girl disappearing beneath the low ceiling of bared pipes and cables; Pennsylvania Station was in the discordant throes of reconstruction. The young man appeared to be going after her, but nobody bothered, or took particular notice.

The driver leaned into his cab, picked up the off-white glove and slapped it against his hand, until both man and girl were out of sight. He said aloud :

"It's no skin off my nose."

He climbed back into his seat and started the engine. Not far along, a traffic policeman was controlling the steady flow of taxis and private cars; he was an elderly, grey-haired man who looked tired and weary in his blue-grey uniform; the revolver sticking out of his belt was only the flourish of a regulation outfit. The taxi driver slowed down alongside him.

"Hi, Sam."

"Hi, Andy."

"You see that?"

"What am I supposed to see?"

"That guy who got out of a moving sedan."

"I guess he didn't want to miss his train."

The taxi driver asked : "What train?"

The policeman shrugged, then shouted at a couple of drivers, who were coming along too fast. The taxi driver, glove still in his hand, shrugged and eased off his brakes; but he was hemmed in. He glanced towards the main hall of the embryo new station, torn between curiosity, a sense of danger for the girl, and the need to keep out of trouble.

As he waited, a man got out of a taxi which had pulled up just in front of him.

He was tall and good-looking, and unostentatiously English in his dark grey tweeds and brogues. His eyes were brown, and surprisingly bright as he glanced keenly up and down, his gaze finally settling on the dismantled entrance

to the station. For a moment he stood rigidly locked in some
kind of tension, then suddenly his whole body relaxed and
he smiled. The smile gave him a cavalier brightness, as,
watched by his own cabby and the policeman, he stepped
towards the driver of the girl's taxi.

"Hallo," he said in a deep, English voice. "Have you seen
a black Chrysler sedan in the past minute or two?"

"Sure have."

The stranger's eyes seemed to brighten still more.

"Did a young man get out, in a hurry?"

"Sure did."

"Where did he go?"

"That way," the taxi driver said, and as he spoke he
moved his left arm, touching the window. He was still holding the glove, and the Englishman looked at it with sudden
attention. Even the policeman, impatient with anything
which blocked the carriageway, eyed it interestedly.

"Did you have a girl passenger, just now?" the stranger
asked.

Startled, the driver said: "So if I did?"

"A blonde, wearing a honey-brown suit and pale doeskin gloves?" The Englishman stared at the single glove.

"Why, I sure had me a passenger like that!" the taxi
driver exclaimed.

"Say, mister —" began the traffic policeman.

The Englishman seemed to do three things in the same
moment. He thrust a bill into the hand of the driver who
had brought him, gave another to the driver who held the
glove; and he took the glove away.

"I'll give this to her," he promised. "She'll be very grateful to you."

He smiled again as he turned away, moving with ease
and speed. Half a dozen women glanced at him, and a
pretty young girl turned to stare. He disappeared into the
mass of scaffolding, bricks, cement and lumber which filled

the huge circular entrance to the station. A hundred or more people were in sight, most weighed down with suitcases, and his gaze touched them all as he sought the man he had followed; or the girl who had lost a glove.

It was exactly one minute past five p.m. by the big clock over the ticket offices.

The girl who had lost the glove stood by one of the windows of the ticket office, trying to restrain both impatience and fear. She carried the briefcase under one arm, as if nervous of losing it; now and again she glanced over her shoulder. A middle-aged woman behind her was shifting from one foot to the other with weary impatience, the glance of a man at the next window raked her up and down, coming to rest on the gentle line of her bosom. A rotund commercial traveller seemed unable to keep his eyes from swivelling towards her face. The woman ahead of her, buying a ticket, had launched into a hundred-and-one trifling questions, and under her breath, the girl muttered: "Oh, do *hurry up!*"

As if hearing her, the woman collected her change and sidled away. A sharp-faced male clerk in shirt sleeves looked at the girl, without speaking.

"I want —" she began, in an English voice—then, suddenly, she broke off. A man had appeared within her line of vision—the young, lightly built man who had so affected the taxi driver.

"What do you want?" the clerk asked flatly.

She moistened her lips.

"I want a ticket to Chicago, please."

"On the Broadway Limited?"

The girl, watching the young man, saw the furtive, sly look he shot towards her.

"I'm sorry, I didn't hear you."

"Make up your mind, miss," the clerk said. "Do you want to go by the Broadway Limited?"

"Is that—is that a good train?"

"Is it —" the clerk began, aghast, and then he stated simply : "It's the world's best."

"I'd like a first class ticket, please." The girl glanced round, but the young man had moved out of sight.

"You from England?" the clerk inquired, with sudden interest.

"Yes."

"They do things different over there," he announced, forgivingly. "I can sell you a coach car ticket, but you'll need a Pullman or a bedroom—unless you want to sit up all night."

She looked at him, with quite beautiful grey eyes.

"I'm sorry," she said, in a low-pitched voice, "but I—I've had rather a shock. What time does the train get to Chicago?"

"Nine o'clock, ma'am."

"Tonight?"

"Now listen," the clerk protested, "it's close on nine hundred miles. Are you sure you want to go to Chicago?"

"Oh, yes," she said hurriedly. "I've—I've friends there. Did you say a bedroom?"

"Yes, ma'am."

"By myself?"

"For your exclusive use, surely."

"I'd like one," she decided. She opened her handbag, then her purse, and eased out a thick wad of bills. "How much will it be?"

"Ninety dollars ninety-two cents."

She pulled out two fifty-dollar bills with great deliberation.

The clerk fed a ticket into the machine, then lifted a telephone, spoke briskly, wrote down some numbers, and after a few seconds gave the girl the ticket, the bedroom slip and her change.

"Leaving six o'clock, ma'am. Track nine," he said.

"Thank you." She moved on, then paused to slip the change into her bag. As she did so, the young man who had jumped out of the black Chrysler appeared at her elbow. He looked down at her, half-smiling—a smile that carried no amusement, no reassurance.

"Okay," he grated, "I'll have it." He stretched a hand towards the briefcase, but the girl swung sharply away from him, clutching it to her.

The man moved swiftly after her, gripping her arm with strong, vice-like fingers.

"You've forgotten your father haven't you?" he muttered under his breath. "If you don't want to make a lot of trouble for the guy, you'll act normal—and you'll let me have that case."

The girl gasped, as if something close to terror touched her.

"Where is he?"

"Just give me the briefcase and he'll sleep easier tonight," the man said. He made a swift darting movement, snatching the case from her. "Listen, you. Don't talk to anyone—to the police, or anyone. Don't even say you lost this, just forget it. Go back to England on the first flight you can make. Otherwise the world will know your father and stolen goods go together. Understand me?"

He moved away without waiting for a reply, the briefcase gripped firmly beneath his arm.

The girl stood staring after him.

The crowds of passengers surged backwards and forwards, each person intent on his own business; no one appeared to have witnessed what had just happened, or if they had, no one appeared to care. Nobody approached, nobody spoke, as the girl watched the young man who had taken the briefcase stride quickly away.

Suddenly, another man, a stranger to the girl, barged heavily into him.

This second man was dressed in grey tweeds, and was tall and powerful; the younger one reeled away, and then began to stagger. Almost at the same moment, the tall man turned out of the main hall, moving very fast. The girl hardly realised what had happened, and yet there was the evidence of her eyes. The *tall* man now had the briefcase, and the other was still trying to regain his balance. The girl began to run after the new owner, but as she did so a red-capped porter touched her arm.

"This is for you, miss," he said, and held out a slip of paper. She brushed it aside distractedly, but the porter persisted. "Please read this, miss," he pleaded, and she looked down and saw a note printed in block capitals. It was almost impossible not to read:

GO ON TO CHICAGO—YOU'LL GET YOUR CASE BACK THERE.

CHAPTER TWO

Broadway Limited

THE man who had taken the case was out of sight.

The young man who had stolen it from the girl had recovered his balance, and was standing irresolute, hands clenched, looking first in one direction, then the other.

The porter asked in a soft and gentle voice :

"Are you all right, miss?"

After a pause, the girl answered : "Yes. Yes, thank you." She knew she would never be able to find the man who now had the briefcase, whom she had seen only for a moment, yet she had this message, a promise that she would get it back in Chicago—where she had planned to meet her father.

"Can I help you?" the porter asked with soft-voiced persistence.

"The train called The Broadway Limited, is it in, do you know?"

"It's loading right now at track nine, miss. You can go aboard any time you wish."

"I'd like to go at once," she said, but hesitated, watching the young man swing round, scowling, and rush out of the hall in what was surely futile pursuit. He disappeared. "Yes, I would like to go at once," the girl repeated, more firmly.

"Is your baggage on board, miss?"

She thought : "Baggage?" and then added hastily, to save explanations : "Yes. Yes, it is ."

"Then you go right on that train," repeated the porter, pointing. "Down that slope, right there. You can't miss it."

She walked quickly towards a barrier where a red notice-board said BROADWAY LIMITED—SIX P.M., and went down a long flight of steps at the foot of which three uniformed men were standing on a poorly-lit platform; this was rather like an underground station. The men were talking at the side of a huge silvery train; even in her preoccupation the girl noticed that all three had white carnations in their buttonholes. She hovered by them.

"What car do you want?" one man inquired.

"Car?"

"Do you have a ticket?"

"Yes, of course." She took the ticket from her handbag, aware that the three were watching her, probably curious because she kept looking back up the steps. One man took her ticket, glanced at it, and said:

"Car 178, miss—right next to the diner. Two cars that-away." He pointed.

She walked along the platform, mammoth silvered carriages towering above her. Even in its own right, this subterranean part of the station—which seemed so dark with its enormous cars, the wheels and undercarriages of which were on a level with her waist—would have been strange and alarming; now it added to her apprehension and to the shock of what had happened.

Another porter, very dark-skinned, looked at her and asked off-handedly:

"What car, miss?"

"Number 178, please."

"Okay. What bedroom?"

"I—I'm not sure." She handed him the ticket.

"That's okay, miss—Room H. Just follow me." Slow moving, he led the way up the iron steps, into the carriage, along a narrow corridor. Two or three doors were open, including one with a sign outside it saying 'H'. "How about your baggage, miss?"

"I—I haven't any."

"You mean it ain't arrived yet?"

What was the use of trying to explain that she had come here at a minute's notice, not daring to go back to her hotel room, where her luggage was? Once again she took the line of least resistance, saying:

"I hope it will catch up with me soon."

"I'll bring it right along, miss." The porter turned away, leaving her alone in a tiny bedroom with metal walls, two chairs, innumerable lights and switches and gadgets; everything was painted grey-green. The blind at the window was down, and she pulled it up to see a porter trundling a large truck, crammed full of suitcases. The station looked gloomy and dirty, and also very different from an English station. Feeling suddenly homesick for familiar things, she closed the narrow door and dropped into a chair.

Exhaustion overwhelmed her, for she had flown from England only that morning, and for a few moments she leaned back, her eyes closed. Then, drowsily, she opened her bag and took out the printed note the porter had given her:

GO ON TO CHICAGO—YOU'LL GET YOUR CASE BACK THERE.

The man who had taken the case must have felt absolutely sure he would get it from the thief, to write such a note beforehand. How had he known about the case? Who was he? A vague picture of a handsome man with an easy smile hovered in her mind's eye—and then she fell asleep.

When she woke, the train was moving.

She started up, astonished, leaned forward and pulled up the blind. Beyond a black void was a peppering of tiny, very bright lights. The train did not seem to be going very fast, it's motion remaining smooth and comfortable. She glanced at her watch.

It was after eight o'clock.

"I can't believe it," she said aloud. "Goodness! I'm even hungry!"

She felt rested, and surprisingly free from depression as she began to look about her. A narrow door led to a tiny W.C. compartment, a handbasin opened out of the side of the carriage by the window, paper cups were in a metal holder close to a tap marked ICE WATER. She ran some, childishly delighted to find that it *was* ice cold. For the first time, she felt a touch of exhilaration, anxiety was shelved to the back of her mind. She could even think composedly of last night's transatlantic telephone call from her father, his request for her to bring him the packet in the briefcase, her hurried telephoning to arrange the flight by B.O.A.C. VC-10, another telephone call from her father soon after she had reached the New York hotel to which he had told her to go.

"Did you bring the packet, Ethel?"

"Yes, of course."

"I can't come to New York, after all, I'm sorry. If I did, I would be exposed to unnecessary danger. I want you to bring it to me in Chicago—I'm staying there for a few days before flying to San Antonio. Get here as soon as you can, and come by train. Is that clear?"

"Yes. But Daddy —"

"Don't worry, now. Just bring it. When you arrive in Chicago, telephone this number . . ."

It had all been mysterious, a little worrying, even exciting—until the young man who had later followed her to the station and stolen the briefcase, had tapped at the door of her hotel room and tried to force his way in.

She pushed the thought of both encounters out of her mind, touched her hair, and went into the passage. The porter, hatless and unrecognisable, was coming out of a compartment a few doors along.

"Your baggage didn't arrive, miss." It was a dirge-like complaint.

"I can manage. Where is the dining-car, please?"

He showed her the way.

Soon, she was studying the menu, writing down what she wanted on an order form, listening to the soft, warming voices of the stewards, intrigued by the polish of the cutlery and the snow-white linen, the ebb and flow of diners, the steady movement of the train. Twice it stopped, but she did not pay much attention.

It was half-past nine when she asked for her bill—"Your check, ma'am," her waiter corrected her smilingly. She paid him, and made her way back along the corridor. Opening her compartment door, she saw that the bed had been pulled away from the wall and made up. She could go to bed at once, if she wanted to. At least there was no need to worry about undressing; she need only slip off her suit, take off her shoes and stockings, and that would be that. She didn't relish going to bed without brushing her teeth, but managed an improvised toilet fairly adequately. In five minutes she lay with the sheet over her. The events of the day drifted through her mind, dream and nightmare over-lapping. She thought more and more of the handsome man who had taken the briefcase; she could picture his smile in her mind's eye.

There was a small light, close to the bed. She touched the switch, and it turned from white to blue, so that she could just see about the room. Soon, she began to doze again, lulled by the movement of the train.

Suddenly, a shadow loomed over her : black; menacing.

In a surge of terror, she opened her mouth to scream. But there was no chance to scream.

A man's hand clamped down over her mouth, making her gulp for breath. She began to choke.

"Quiet!" he breathed. "Quiet."

Her breast was heaving, she felt as if she would suffocate.

"Quiet!" he repeated, slapping her stingingly across her cheek.

She lay on her back, gasping for breath, seeing the sly face of the young man who had first stolen the briefcase, taking on a demoniac glow in the pale blue light. His hand pressed against her throat, seeming to threaten greater pressure. He shifted his position, so that he could sit on the edge of the bed. One hand was heavy on her shoulder, the other on her neck.

"If you shout, I'll choke the life out of you," he threatened.

She didn't attempt to reply.

"Understand?"

She nodded, in sharp alarm.

"Don't forget. Who was the guy who took the briefcase from me?"

"I—I don't know."

"Don't lie to me, you silly bitch!"

She shook her head helplessly.

"Listen," the man said viciously, "I'll choke the life out of you if you don't tell me." He pressed more heavily against her, and she believed he might carry out his threat. She hated the touch of his hands and felt nauseated, but she stayed motionless. He leaned forward, his face very close to hers, and she could feel his breath against her skin. "*Who was he?* Answer me!"

"I—I tell you I don't know!"

"Listen," the man said in a rasping voice, "I can do what I like with you. I've got a knife. I could lay your cheeks open, so you'd be scarred for life. Or I could put one of your eyes out."

Her breath hissed between her teeth.

"*Don't!*"

"*Who is the guy?*"

He would never believe that she did not know, and if she continued to tell the truth, he might do unspeakable things to her. She remembered her father's voice on the telephone. "If I did, I would be exposed to unnecessary danger —"

The man's hands were pressing harder, and she found it more and more difficult to breathe; his mouth was only inches from hers when he repeated :

"Tell me who he is."

What could she say to make him ease the pressure? What could possibly convince him? She sought desperately for something, and then burst out :

"He's a friend of my father !"

"What's his name?"

She hadn't anticipated the question, she didn't know what to say.

"I — I don't know !"

He drew back, giving her a moment of exquisite relief, and then slapped her again across the face, sharply enough to hurt as if his hand were red-hot. It made her cry out — and made her strike out instinctively. She would never know how it happened, but her tormentor slipped, and fell to the floor, with a thud. As she realised what had happened, she sat up quickly, snatched her pillow from behind her, and struck at him as he tried to get up. The blow shot him backwards again. She saw the lighting switch panel and drew her palm down it; light after light clicked on, vivid bright. The man on the floor was as dazzled as she. She put a hand to her eyes.

"If you don't go, I'll call the porter !"

"Why, you little bitch, I —"

"I'll call him, I tell you !"

The man raised himself on his elbow, raking her with a glance she hated. She became acutely aware that she was wearing only a flimsy slip. He began to get up, very slowly, fixing his gaze on her breast; the way his lips moved, the red wetness of them, told her what was in his mind.

She gripped the pillow tightly with one hand, and stretched out towards the call-button with the other.

"If you do that," the man said, "your father won't live the week out."

She winced.

"And if I don't get the briefcase back, neither of you will live," he threatened, his gaze still raking her up and down. "That would be a bad deal, you could give a lot of guys a lot of pleasure."

Surprisingly calmly, she said: "You're a dirty-minded beast. Don't move." There was just room to squeeze past him, to a bigger space near the wash-basin, so that he was between her and the door, with his back to it. "Get out," she ordered.

"Your father —"

"My father can look after himself. So can I."

She was far enough away from him to feel safer; now that she was standing up she believed she could cope, even the threat to her father troubled her less. If this man would only leave her alone —

The man was getting slowly, warily, to his feet.

If he went out she could bolt the door—why *had* she forgotten to bolt it when she went to bed?—and so be safe until the morning; gaining such a respite seemed the only thing that mattered. But would he go? Or was he planning some new kind of attack, seeking a way to put her off her guard?

He was on his feet again, and had only to lunge forward to reach her. But as his hand swept round to slap her—hard enough to knock her back against the bed—the compartment door swung open and a man stood framed in the doorway.

It was the man who had taken the briefcase.

CHAPTER THREE

Knife by Night

BEFORE the girl's assailant had time to turn, the newcomer dropped his hands on to the other's shoulders. Gripping hard, he began to shake him, with greater and greater violence, until his victim's head jerked to and fro, his breath coming in broken gasps. There was grimness on the newcomer's face. His brown eyes were hard and relentless, his lips set tightly.

At last the shaking stopped.

The newcomer pushed his victim back into the bedroom, manœuvring him so that he collapsed on to the bed. His eyes were rolling and his mouth was slack; saliva dribbled from one corner.

On the instant, the stranger's expression changed. He smiled at the girl, and slipped a hand into his pocket, pulling out the doeskin glove he had taken from the taxi-driver. He held it towards her.

"I think you dropped this. Your briefcase is quite safe, by the way—but I think I'd better keep it until we get to Chicago. Our friend here"—he nodded towards the unconscious man—"might have an accomplice."

The girl took the glove. "Thank you," she said gravely. She laid it across the back of the chair, hesitated for a moment, then looked directly into the stranger's eyes. "Who are you?" she asked simply.

"My name is Mannering. John Mannering."

"I'm Ethel Alundo."

"Professor Arthur Alundo's daughter?"

"How on earth did you guess?"

"It isn't the most common name," said John Mannering dryly. "And Professor Alundo is a most uncommon person."

"Do you know him?"

"No. I've often wanted to meet him."

"Then you may be able to in Chicago," Ethel Alundo remarked. "Or San Antonio."

John Mannering closed the compartment door as he asked: "What made you say San Antonio?"

"Because he's going there for the opening of some big exhibition, or whatever it's called."

Mannering smiled faintly.

"The HemisFair, I believe." He did not explain how he came to know, but glanced again at the man on the bed. "Do you know *his* name?"

"No."

"He is Enrico Ballas," Mannering told her quietly.

"I don't think I've ever heard of him," said Ethel Alundo, half-frowning.

"You would remember if you had," Mannering said, dryly. "He is an unusual mixture of jewel connoisseur, thief, and —" he paused, before articulating the next words with great precision: "Knife-artist." After another pause, he went on: "Do you know what a knife-artist is?"

Slowly, as if perplexed, the girl answered: "A man who uses a knife as a weapon?"

"A man who uses a knife as a means of torture," Mannering corrected.

Ethel shuddered. "How horrible."

"He is horrible. He comes from horrible stock. And for the rest of time, he will hate us both: me, because I have humiliated him; you, because you have witnessed that humiliation."

Ethel didn't answer.

"I can look after myself, but you —" Mannering looked

at the girl's slender frame reflectively. "Ethel, do you know the significance of what I'm saying?"

"Yes," she answered. "I think so, anyway."

The peculiar thing was the calmness with which she accepted Mannering's warning that from this moment on she would be in danger from Enrico Ballas—danger of injury, of being scarred for life. Ballas would hate her; from the first moment she had seen him she had recognised his capacity for hatred; for evil.

Mannering looked at her almost sternly.

"You must never take any chances with Enrico Ballas."

"I shall certainly try not to," she assured him.

"Or anyone of the same name," Mannering went on. "There is an older Ballas, Enrico's uncle, who is very jealous of his family's honour."

"You make him sound as if he's as bad as his nephew."

"Some say that he is worse," said Mannering.

"Do you know him?"

"Not personally," Mannering answered. "We've had business dealings, that's all."

Enrico Ballas was still lying in a huddle on the bed, but there was tension in his body, a stiffening of his arms and legs. Mannering noticed this when he glanced down, and so did the girl; but Mannering did nothing and made no comment. In fact his smile seemed even more relaxed as he said :

"That's good. When did you first come across him?"

"This morning. Mr. Mannering —"

"Where?"

"At my hotel. Mr. Mannering —"

"Why did he come to see you?"

Ethel drew in her breath. "Mr. Mannering, who *are* you?"

As she asked the question, she saw the change in Mannering's expression, saw him swing round, saw the flash of steel in Ballas's hand the glint of malevolence in his eyes. His body was convulsed, the knife with its vicious-looking, pointed blade stabbed towards Mannering. Mannering struck the wrist of the hand holding the knife and, with his other hand, struck Enrico Ballas on the chin. There was a sharp crack of sound, and Ballas fell limply back on the bed.

The knife lay on the floor: shimmering.

"You have to give him full marks for trying," Mannering said dryly. "Would you care to get dressed while I deal with him?"

For the first time since Mannering had entered the bedroom, Ethel Alundo remembered the inadequacy of her clothing. She flushed, caught a glimpse of laughter in Mannering's eyes, laughed herself—and then saw him turn his back and bend over the man whom he had knocked out. He was still bending over Ballas as she finished dressing, and she watched, fascinated. He had taken the man's shoes off, and his trousers; he had tied the trousers about the other's legs, at the knees, using each leg as a rope. Now he took off the man's jacket and went through the pockets, dropping the contents on to the bed—a wallet, a key, handkerchief, comb, some tickets, two ballpoint pens, and some loose change. As he finished examining the jacket, he glanced round.

"Care to lend a hand?"

"Of course."

"While I hold him in a sitting position, you put his jacket on back to front, and button it up."

"Back to —" Ethel began, and then her voice rose. "Oh! Like a straight-jacket."

She fastened the buttons with quick efficiency, and Mannering laid Ballas down, punching a pillow into position beneath his head. Then he picked up a white handkerchief and tied it round his prisoner's head and face.

"Not that he's likely to shout even if he could," Mannering said. "I doubt if he wants to be found by the train crew. But just in case." He turned to Ethel. "Are you all right?"

Faintly, Ethel said : "Oh, I'm fine."

"I've got a compartment in the next car," Mannering told her. "Let's go and talk there."

Leaving her own compartment with some relief, Ethel followed Mannering as he led the way in the opposite direction to the dining-car. At a door marked E he stopped, but he did not immediaely open it. Instead, he put his ear close to the metal, kept it there for an appreciable time, drew back, opened the door slowly, and then sent it crashing back. Nothing stirred. He went inside, looking swiftly round him before beckoning to her.

"I'm sorry to be so melodramatic," he apologised, "but Enrico Ballas has friends and allies as well as relations."

Ethel made no comment.

The bed, she noticed, was not made, and two easy chairs stood by the wide blind-covered window. He motioned her to one, then took out a slim, gold cigarette case.

"Will you have a cigarette?"

"No, thank you."

"Do you smoke?"

"Very seldom."

"Would you care for a whisky?"

She hesitated.

"Is it easy to get?"

"Nothing easier." Mannering drew a small leather case from beneath the bed, and opened it; inside were four flasks. He touched one, looked up, and asked : "Would you prefer brandy?"

"I think I would. I need—*some*thing to steady my nerves."

She was looking at him out of clear, light grey eyes, very intently. The line of her face was a little too long for real beauty, he noticed, yet there was beauty in her.

He handed her a glass, and she sipped, appreciatively, before she asked :

"Mr. Mannering, how long were you outside the door?"

"I followed our friend along the passage. When I saw him go into your compartment I waited to see if you needed any help."

"And you allowed that beast to jump at me, to frighten the wits out of me?" Indignation sparked in the grey eyes.

"I had to find out what you were talking about," Mannering admitted gravely.

"You knew he'd taken the briefcase from me. You must have realised how frightened I was on the station!"

"Or how cleverly you pretended to be," Mannering murmured.

"Pretended?"

"If he had wanted me to regard you as a damsel in distress, he could hardly have done it better," reasoned Mannering. "I had to be quite sure that it wasn't all an act put on to make me believe you were very sweet and trustworthy."

"Are you seriously telling me that you thought *I* might be—be an accomplice of that man?"

"The thought had crossed my mind."

"Well, I am not!"

"After hearing the conversation in your room I feel sure your not," said Mannering. "But I had to *make* sure. And now I'll tell you what you need to know about me. I am an antique dealer, and also deal in *objets d'art* and jewels. Occasionally I am consulted by the police; and occasionally clients, who don't want the police to know they have been robbed, ask me to investigate losses for them. I followed Enrico Ballas from London to New York because I thought he had stolen two valuable pieces of jewellery from one of these clients. He gave me the slip in the Grand Park Hotel. Is that where you were staying in New York?"

"Yes," Ethel said, and her eyes were growing wider. "Are you *the* John Mannering? The man who's called the Baron?"

"The truth will out," Mannering said, wryly.

She stared at him, wonderingly.

"You're quite *famous*."

"So is Professor Arthur Alundo."

"I mean —"

"Be an angel, and forget it," Mannering said. "I caught up with Ballas at an apartment on Park Avenue, just as he was leaving. I followed him—and saw you come out of the hotel and get into a taxi. Directly afterwards he came tearing out, and asked a doorman which way you'd gone. I followed—that's how I happened to be at Pennsylvania Station." Mannering's eyes positively danced as he went on: "I wondered if those stolen jewels were in your briefcase."

"They're not!"

"I know. I've looked."

Quite spontaneously, Ethel burst out laughing; and Mannering chuckled with her. He had a way with him which not only intrigued but enchanted her, and she was more than ever aware of his attractiveness. He was in the middle-forties, she guessed—but with his dark hair and slightly tanned skin, fine eyes and regular features, the middle years did not weigh heavily on him.

"Would you mind telling me your story?" he asked.

She realised that was just what she wanted to do. Her faith in a man now revealed to her as a renowned detective, and her alarm for her father, made her talk with great fluency. Mannering lay back in his chair, glass in hand, listening to her pleasing voice, noticing the way her expression changed as she talked, now showing fear, now alarm, now anger, now apprehension. She could not be more than twenty-one or two, he felt sure, and in some ways she had the naïveté of a child in her early teens; in others, she was a mature woman.

One thing seemed certain: she was very much afraid for that remarkable man, her father.

CHAPTER FOUR

Coincidence?

AT last, the whole story was told.

Mannering had listened without interruption, watching Ethel's alert young face, understanding something of her emotions; yet he remained a little puzzled. She was obviously greatly worried about her father; on the other hand she seemed to disapprove of him. She was affectionate towards him, but there was a note of exasperation in the way she spoke, as when she said : "There's absolutely *no* telling where he'll be off to next." When she had finished she leaned forward and stretched out her hands.

"Will *you* help, Mr. Mannering?"

"Yes, of course," Mannering said. "Let me go over what you've told me, to make sure I have it right."

"That's a good idea."

Mannering stretched his legs out as he, in turn, began to talk. The story went back for six months, to the April of that year, when Professor Alundo had come to America to give a series of Peace Lectures at most of the major cities of the United States. Some of the lectures were at universities, some at political meetings of both Democratic and Republican parties. The one in San Antonio was to be at the Political Centre of the exhibition known as the HemisFair, which was due to open in a week's time. As far as Ethel had known, he had left England with no particular anxieties. A widower for several years, a Doctor of Philosophy who had gradually acquired a worldwide reputation for idealism with a strong leavening of practical commonsense, he had learned to live and travel by himself.

A letter written from Los Angeles, three weeks before Ethel had flown to New York, had given the first hint of trouble. The Professor had said ". . . I am a little worried by some telephone calls, obviously from people who have little goodwill towards me, and I cannot imagine what I may have said or done to create such malice."

Mannering quoted, word for word.

Ethel leaned forward : "What an incredible memory you have !"

"It works sometimes," Mannering said dryly. "After that you had a card from San Francisco, which said nothing of this anxiety, only where he would be next. Then came the telephone call last night."

"At half-past ten. It's hard to believe it *was* only last night, it seems weeks —" She broke off. "I'm sorry."

"You hadn't expected the call. You were at your London flat, working late on some designs for magazine pictures, and were exasperated by the interruption—until you realised who was calling." Or even after she had realised, Mannering reflected. "Your father sounded agitated, and asked you to get a packet from the safe at his flat in Knightsbridge, the keys of which were already in your charge. He told you to go to the Grand Park Hotel, on Park Avenue, near 51st Street, and said that he had already booked you in. Almost as soon as you arrived, he telephoned for you to bring the briefcase to Chicago. You are to call a number he gave you as soon as you get there."

Again, Ethel said in a wondering voice: "You remember *every* detail."

"Is this right, so far?"

"Absolutely."

"What did he sound like on the telephone today?"

After a pause, Ethel said : "Preoccupied."

"Is that normal?"

"Oh, yes," said Ethel. "Unless he's lecturing, or talking

shop, he's the most preoccupied man imaginable. Exasperatingly so, sometimes! He kept breaking off, and—well, he sounded as if he was thinking about two things at once and finding it difficult to keep them separate in his mind. He even kept me waiting for a few moments while he checked the telephone number."

"What is the number?"

Ethel opened her bag, took out a slip of paper, and read: "Whitehall 4–31495."

"Whitehall 4–31495," Mannering echoed. "That's pretty near, if it's not inside, the Loop."

"The Loop?"

"It's easier to show you that, than explain it," Mannering said. "It's an area surrounded by Chicago's overhead railway. Did he say why he wanted you to go by train?"

"No."

"Was he in Chicago?"

"Yes. He said he was staying there for a few days before flying to San Antonio."

"Was he due in Chicago on his itinerary?"

"I don't think so—at least, not until after San Antonio. But I'm not certain. Oh, what a fool I am!"

"In what way?" inquired Mannering, lightly.

"For not bringing a copy of the itinerary with me. Not that it would help if I had," Ethel added ruefully. "My bags are still in New York."

"We'll get them sent by air to Chicago," Mannering interrupted. "That won't be difficult. Let's go on. While you were in your New York hotel room, Enrico Ballas came to see you."

She looked uneasy as she nodded.

"He wanted to know why you were in America, whether you had brought anything for your father," Mannering went on. "You told him you'd come to see friends, that your father had no idea you were here, and you thought you'd persuaded Ballas that this was true. As soon as he'd gone, you yourself left carrying only the briefcase. Is that right?"

"Yes—but it didn't fool him."

"No," Mannering agreed. "Enrico wouldn't work alone, and he would have had you followed. I haven't any doubt he realised you were on your way to Pennsylvania Station—or heading that way—and rushed after you. Do you know what's in the packet?" he added, almost casually.

"I haven't the faintest idea."

"Did you know your father had any secret? Or any valuable documents?"

"No."

"Have you any idea at all what this is about?"

"No," Ethel answered. "I can't begin to imagine. Those malicious telephone calls he said he had didn't really surprise me—he's always saying things which annoy people. He annoys me sometimes. Fanatics can be so blind, and he *is* a fanatic. But—well, I'm completely in the dark over this. Didn't you say *you* looked in the package?"

"Yes."

"What was in it?"

"A box containing some lecture notes which in turn contained some microfilm."

"*Micro*film! But I thought —" Ethel broke off.

"That such stuff was only for spies," Mannering said dryly. "There are a thousand-and-one uses for it, practically all important. Your father's film had been cut in strips, each strip packed close to the margin between each sheet of the notes. They couldn't be seen until I pulled the sheets apart. Did your father always prepare his lectures and have them typed out?"

"Yes—he—Mr. Mannering!" Alarm flared through Ethel.

"What's the trouble?" asked Mannering.

"You said : '*did* he'."

"Did I?"

"Yes. In the past tense."

"Oh," said Mannering, blankly; then he went on quickly: "Yes, I did—but it was a slip of the tongue. I haven't the faintest reason to believe that anything serious has happened to your father. I told you the simple truth, Ethel. I came after Ballas because I wanted to get some jewels back from him. They were stolen a week ago from this client of mine, and I had good reason to believe that Ballas was the thief. It all fitted in very nicely, actually, because I was coming to America anyway."

Ethel looked her 'why?'

"There's to be a display of pre-Columbian artefacts at the San Antonio Fair, and I've a small collection myself," Mannering said. "The authorities asked me to lend it for the Fair, and invited me to go with it."

"So you and Daddy will be there at the same time," remarked Ethel. "It's a remarkable coincidence, isn't it?"

"That I should be after Enrico Ballas and he should be after you?" Mannering pondered. "In a way, I suppose it is, but I've known many stranger ones." He paused before going on: "Except that I know of your father's reputation, this is all absolutely new to me. Enrico Ballas is well-known as a very clever jewel-thief. I knew he was in London and this particular theft had his hallmark. I simply put two and two together."

Ethel laid a hand on Mannering's arm. "You *will* help him, won't you? My father, I mean. He's a really remarkable man, quite remarkable, but he's so—so pig-*headed* over wanting peace at any price that nearly everyone hates —" She broke off, and tears welled up in her eyes.

"Hates this alleged belief," Mannering said gently.

"You know him well enough to say 'alleged'?" Ethel asked, her voice changing with new interest. "*He* swears he *doesn't* believe in peace at any price—but most people think he does."

"I only know that I don't care much for many of the people whom I know oppose him most strongly."

"That's one way of looking at it," she said, broodingly. She frowned in concentration. "*Micro*film?"

"Yes."

"Could he —" The words were almost inaudible.

"Could he have become so frustrated by events that he would do something outrageous for what he believes in?" Mannering asked gently. "Do you think that he might, Ethel?"

She said very slowly : "It wouldn't really surprise me."

"Has he ever suggested —"

"Before he left England he was more evasive than I'd ever known him," Ethel declared. "And he got angrier than ever with people whom he said didn't understand. But I wasn't deeply interested. Not really. I feel a beast, saying so, but I hadn't much patience with him, or rather, with his ideas. I tried not to show it, but he knew. I thought he spent too much time and money he couldn't afford worrying about the world's problems. He writes letters by the hundred, is forever having pamphlets printed. He always seems to think he's the *only* one who can solve the world's problems."

"I know the feeling," Mannering said quietly.

"*You* do?" she marvelled. "But I thought you were just a wealthy dealer in precious things who liked play —" She broke off, embarrassment in her voice.

"Playing at being a detective," Mannering finished for her, his eyes crinkling. "Actually I don't like detecting as much as all that. I find myself acting detective for people who can't do it for themselves but don't want to go to the police. It fills a need." He stopped, watching her intently and questioningly.

Slowly, Ethel said : "*You* take on *other* people's problems, too."

"That's what my wife always says. I don't really agree with her. I agree with your father—any man who sees a thing is wrong ought to try to put it right. Your father's taken on the world and I've taken on a few spendthrift millionaires who break the rules, and really don't deserve help."

Almost shocked, Ethel said : "But you've never met him !"

"Not until we meet in Chicago !"

"And you know him better than *I* do!" Ethel sprang to her feet. "Oh, I feel *dreadful*. He's always been on his own. He's had to fight and fight and fight. All the *right* people call him a Communist and all the Communists call him a warmonger. And he hasn't even been able to rely on help from me. No one's really helped him since my mother died."

"Nonsense," Mannering said.

"It isn't nonsense. At least I know myself."

"I doubt it," said Mannering. "When he needed help he called on you and you dropped everything to do what he wanted. He was quite sure you would. Enough of this wallowing in guilt," he went on briskly. "We'll see him in the morning, and our only real problem is what to do with Enrico Ballas. I ought to send a telegram for your baggage, too. Do you know Chicago?"

"I've never been there."

"We'll have to find time for you to look around," Mannering said. "But don't expect a gangster round every corner !" He raised his head. "We're slowing down, it may be for a station. Stay here in my compartment—and bolt the door."

It wasn't until she had actually pushed the bolt that Ethel realised the implications of the command. Although Mannering had already mentioned the possibility of Enrico Ballas having an accomplice on board the train, the significance of this had not, at the time, struck home. It was clear to her

now that Mannering suspected she may be the victim of yet
a second attack.

Mannering waited to hear the bolt shoot home before
moving away. Reaching the end of the car, where the Pullman porter was waiting to open the door, he slipped a notepad out of his pocket. The dark, round face relaxed into an
approving smile at sight of him.

"Are we going to take on passengers?" Mannering asked.

"Yes, sir."

"How long will we be here?"

"Two or three minutes, sir, no more than that. You won't
have time to leave the train."

"Will there be a Western Union office on the station?"

"There sure will, sir, but you won't have no time —"

Mannering was opening the notepad.

"If I write out a cable, will a red-cap hand it in for
me?"

"Sure be glad to, sir."

"Fine," said Mannering. He drew back, wrote in block
lettering: PLEASE FORWARD MY BAGGAGE AIR
FREIGHT TO CONRAD HILTON HOTEL CHICAGO,
ETHEL ALUNDO, wrapped the message inside a five
dollar bill, and, as soon as the train stopped, jumped out. A
porter holding a trolley with two passengers beside it, was
almost opposite. The two porters handled the baggage, and
Mannering said : "Send this cable for me, will you? And
keep the change."

"Why yes, sir ! I'll be glad to do that for you."

Mannering jumped back into the train, and almost immediately it moved off. He stood on the swaying platform
between two cars, for a few minutes. Enrico Ballas almost
certainly had an accomplice on board, but looking for him
would be a waste of time. There was another way to work;
the accomplice would probably soon come to look for

Enrico, and the most likely place for him to look was in Ethel's compartment. Mannering passed this on the way back to her, tapped on the door of his own compartment, and went in as Ethel opened it. The porter came shuffling along.

"Shall I make up your bed, sir?"

"Yes, please," Mannering said. "I'm going to have a drink in the club car. Ready, Ethel?"

The porter showed no sign of surprise at Ethel's presence.

Half-an-hour later, in an armchair in the club car, she stifled a yawn.

Mannering said: "You'll take my compartment. I'll fix another with the porter." He didn't give her time to argue but guided her back along the corridor, took his pigskin case from the foot of the bed, and carried it along to her original cabin. He opened the door and stepped inside.

Enrico Ballas still lay there.

Mannering pushed a chair into position, and sat down, pondering all that the girl had told him. He thought of the microfilm, too, and began to recall more vividly all he knew of Professor Alundo, then to reflect that it *was* a coincidence that he, the Baron, in an effort to recover Freddy Fentham's family jewels, should be pursuing Ballas, only to find him involved with Alundo. Was Enrico doing two jobs at the same time? Or was he himself wrong in suspecting him guilty of the theft of the jewels?

Now and again footsteps sounded outside the door, and Mannering paused expectantly, until they had passed on.

He began to feel drowsy, repeatedly jerking himself upright. On one such awaking, a spot of dark crimson on the sheet, caught his eye. It stood out vividly against the white, and he wondered how he could have missed it. He leaned forward, eyeing it, and even as he did so the red spread quite perceptibly.

Suddenly, he realised that it was blood.

With this realisation came another!

Someone had come into the compartment, and used a knife on Enrico.

CHAPTER FIVE

"Did You *Kill Ballas?"*

MANNERING moved towards Enrico Ballas, staring search-ingly, reaching for his right arm and the pulse. It was still. The wrist was warm, but there was a hint of the chill of death, and Mannering had no doubt of the truth. He lowered the limp arm carefully, then eased the body so that he could see the position of the wound. Whoever had come in here had pushed the helpless man on to his side, then thrust the knife to the heart. The awful, the unspeakable thing, was that Ballas must have been aware of what was happening. Unable to move or shout, he must have waited for the thrust of death. Even for a killer, that was a dreadful fate.

Until the final realisation came to him, Enrico must have believed that help against Mannering was at hand.

Chilled by the horror of these facts, Mannering backed to the farthest point.

There was no way of disposing of the body unless he carried it to one of the other compartments, and the risk of being seen was too great. Yet thoughts of taking the chance passed in and out of his mind, with other, inescapable facts. This was Ethel Alundo's compartment. Once the body was found here, there would be a hue and cry for her. It might be best to send for the porter now and make a clear statement—that the girl had been frightened by an in-truder, that he—Mannering—had exchanged rooms with her to try to settle her fears, and had come along and found the body. He could say that he had had nothing to do with tying the man up, and Ethel would surely support him —

Would she?

Or would the fact of murder unnerve her?

Quite suddenly, Mannering was faced with a host of questions, none of them easy to answer. Yet there was little time. Was Ethel's story true? Could he rely on her in a crisis? Could he be sure that her father was innocent of espionage, or some other crime? Obviously he couldn't—as obviously, he had no proof that she, either, could be trusted. Yet the fact that such a man as Enrico Ballas had threatened her and taken the briefcase, was surely an argument in her favour.

Nonsense; he wasn't thinking clearly, the shock of discovering that murder had been done had confused him.

First things first —

He *must* get the body out of here, *and* change the sheet and mattress; the police must not suspect him or the girl too soon, whatever the truth about her and her father. Yes, first things first. He leaned over and eased the mattress from the far side, finding that even with the body's dead weight, he could lift it. He let it fall slowly, then stepped into the corridor; no one was in sight. Two compartments along, the door was open, the bed made, but Mannering could see no baggage or clothing. He slipped swiftly into the compartment and lifted the mattress, bedding and all. Clasping the whole conglomeration to his body, like an enormous shield, he stepped boldly back to the dead man's compartment, holding his breath. He had to fumble for the handle, but at last opened the door and managed to get inside unseen.

Breathing hard, he let his load slide to the floor, then, turning round, he hoisted the dead man and the blood-stained mattress, hugging the body to him. He had to bend his head to one side, both to see and to breathe. Staggering into the corridor with this second load, he made his way towards the empty room, but tripped and lost his balance as he squeezed through the doorway. He came up against the window, pressing tightly against the dead man as he did so, squeezing the breath out of his own body.

He recovered, regained his hold, hoisted and pushed the mattress roughly into position, straightened the body on it, then stepped out and closed the door.

As he did so, a man turned into the corridor—stubby cigar jutting from thick square lips. He was tall and heavily built, and wore a tightly fitting suit. Mannering thought he detected an Irish look about him—and perhaps a wary one.

"Good evening."

"Hiyah."

They squeezed past each other, the tobacco foul in Mannering's nostrils.

The man had not glanced into Ethel Alundo's compartment where the clean mattress and bedding lay in a heap on the floor. Mannering closed the door of this compartment from the outside, then went back to the other. It was only a matter of a moment or two to adjust the mattress and the body on it. The blood had spread a little farther on to the sheet, but there was none on the floor; nothing to show— as far as Mannering was able to judge—that the murder had not been committed here.

He returned to Ethel's room, put the clean mattress on the bed, rumpled the sheet, and punched the pillow; at first sight, it now looked as if the bed had been slept in.

This done, he had to go and see Ethel; and in a matter of seconds he had to make up his mind whether to tell her the whole truth, or whether merely to say that he had moved Enrico Ballas from her room to another.

One fact emerged clearly; Ethel was sure to find out about the murder on the train before long. So if he didn't tell her everything now, when she did find out, she might believe that he was the killer.

For all he knew, she might believe this even if he did tell her now.

He tapped at the door, calling in a low voice: "It's me. John Mannering," and in a few moments it opened. Ethel had obviously been asleep. Her hair was tousled, her nose shiny, and she had such a look of youthful innocence that Mannering caught his breath, and for a moment stood with the door open. As he did so, he heard a movement, stepped back into the corridor, and saw the porter, black face lugubrious, big eyes heavy with tiredness, lips set in re-proach.

"You want me to make up your room, sir?"

"Leave it," Mannering said. "I've some work to do."

"Are you sure, sir?"

"Quite sure."

The porter looked puzzled; and when the police ques-tioned him about the passengers in the car, he would re-member the Englishman who had sat up working all night. Mannering watched him shuffle away to an empty room and his own sleep, then went into the compartment.

Ethel had curled up in one of the armchairs. She looked innocence itself.

Mannering chose that moment to remind himself that she could have gone into the other bedroom, and killed Ballas.

The very thought came as a shock, and staring down at her he actually formed the words : *"Could she have done that?"* Acutely aware of the gentle curve of her cheeks, the sweeping lashes, he asked the question again : *Could she have killed Ballas?* And he made himself answer the ques-tion as a policeman would : Yes, she had had the oppor-tunity, when he had been arranging for the cable to be sent; she might even have a motive—in fact she *had* a motive, for the dead man had threatened her father.

Watching the rhythmic rise and fall of her bosom, he realised she had gone back to sleep.

Mannering took off his tie, slipped off his shoes and loosened his belt, then sat back in the other armchair. It wasn't exactly comfortable, but soon the jolting of the train and the sound of the wheels on the rails, strangely muted, began to make him feel drowsy.

Now and again, he stirred, but he did not wake until daylight showed at the cracks by the sides of the blind. He straightened up, feeling a crick in his neck, and then looked towards the girl. She was curled up in her chair, just as she had been last night, but her eyes were open, and she was staring at him.

He ran a forefinger over his stubble, and moistened his lips. It was warm in here—too warm for him, although the girl seemed fresh and bright-eyed.

"Good morning," Mannering said. "I'm afraid I'm not at my best in the morning."

"Aren't you?" She smiled, unexpectedly. "You look very good to me."

It was one of the few occasions when Mannering was at a loss for words. He shifted his position and stretched a hand towards the window.

"Can you stand a little more light?"

"Of course."

Raising the blind, he looked through the dusty glass on to a vast stretch of flat land, dotted with trees and one lonely farmhouse. Turning towards Ethel, he saw that she had already combed her hair and straightened her clothes. She was studying him in a speculative way he found a little worrying. She could be most disconcerting, and again he thought fleetingly of the fact that she could have killed Ballas.

Almost as if she 'saw' the name in his mind, she asked:

"Shouldn't one of us go and see that man?"

Mannering straightened up, hesitated, and decided that the best approach was the direct, even the brutal one.

"He was murdered last night," he announced.

At first he thought she took the news too calmly; that she could not have done so had she not previously been aware of it. Then he realised that the significance of what he had said was dawning on her very slowly. The gradual change in her expression was quite remarkable: from a speculative one touched with disquiet about the man in her bedroom, to shocked disbelief, bewilderment, then horror.

She started up.

"You can't mean that!"

"I went to see how he was, and someone had stabbed him to death."

All the colour was draining from Ethel's cheeks. Mannering half expected protestations and expostulations : It wasn't possible, it couldn't have happened, she didn't believe it!— all those, and more. Instead, she seemed to freeze. The train chugged on, past the unchanging land which lay so monotonously flat as far as the eye could see. A man walked along the corridor; two cars appeared, swift and unexpected, on a road running alongside the track.

Ethel said suddenly :

"What did you do?"

"I put him into an empty compartment."

"Weren't you—*seen*?"

"There's been no alarm, so presumably I wasn't; he can't have been found, either."

There was another long pause, before Ethel asked :

"Why didn't you call the police?"

"Because if I'd called them, I would have had to tell them your story as well as mine." When she didn't respond, he went on: "And if I know policemen, both of us would have been held for questioning." When she still kept silent, he hazarded "I'd prefer to go on to Chicago. Wouldn't you?"

"Yes," Ethel said, almost explosively, "but —"

She caught her breath.

"But what?" Mannering prompted.

"If—if we're caught *now*—won't it look worse?"

"If it could be proved we had known about it—yes."

"*Can* they prove it?"

"Possibly," Mannering said. "It's a question of priorities. Doing our legal duty by the body of Enrico Ballas and society, or finding out what's happened to your father. It's quite likely that Ballas was killed by someone who knew he had lost the briefcase and feared he might be persuaded to give some secret away. His accomplices may not have trusted him, and dared not run the risk of him talking."

A faint colour was seeping back in Ethel's cheeks. She gave a little shudder.

"You make it all sound so cold-blooded.'

"It *is* cold-blooded."

Very slowly, the girl nodded.

"Yes, it is. It certainly is. What do you propose to do?"

"Get off the train as if nothing had happened. If the body's found, lie like a trooper. There's no reason why we should be associated with an American gangster —"

"*Gangster?*"

"Modern version."

"Is he—oh, I suppose it doesn't matter." She waved her hands, almost angrily. "There must have been dozens of people who saw him talking to me at the station."

"That won't be discovered for quite a while—possibly not at all."

"They're *bound* to question us."

"And if they do, we tell them that we were attracted by each other and decided to share a bedroom for the night. No one," added Mannering with a faint smile, "could be surprised to learn that I had been attracted by you."

She looked at him straightly.

"Nor me by you," she rejoined, matter-of-factly. "Mr.— Mr. Mannering, *why* are you taking such risks?"

"I would like to know what that microfilm's about, and I *am* sufficiently attracted by you not to want to see you in trouble with the police." After a pause, while she appeared to be weighing up all he said, he went on : "And I'm prone to this kind of risk—it's like being accident-prone. Also, I was already interested in Ballas, so —"

"I understand all that," Ethel interrupted, as if it was a waste of time to go on talking. "Will you answer me one question?"

"Yes."

"Did *you* kill Ballas?" Ethel Alundo demanded.

After the first shock, Mannering was almost unable to restrain a laugh, because the question was so blunt, and the serious intentness of it so obvious. He checked the laugh but not a smile, and answered :

"No."

After a long pause, while Ethel appeared to be trying to divine the truth, she relaxed a little.

"I'll do whatever you say," she promised.

"Then go along to the dining-car ahead of me," said Mannering. "I'll join you for breakfast in ten minutes."

They had breakfast—and no alarm was raised.

They returned to their compartments—and there was still no alarm.

The train began to slow down on the outskirts of Chicago, the ugly, dirty, dilapidated hovels and backyards which seem to line the railways of every big city. Soon there was a great stirring and calling out, and footsteps in the corridor. Ethel had rejoined Mannering, and now they both stood tight-lipped and silent in Mannering's compartment.

There was no alarm.

They passed the door of the compartment where the body

lay, stepped down on to the platform, two among two hundred; and as they turned in the direction of the station hall, two men in police uniform and two men who were obviously plain-clothes detectives, came striding towards them.

CHAPTER SIX

Chicago—Chicago

MANNERING felt Ethel's fingers tighten on his arm, and glanced down at her. She was looking straight ahead, pale but unfaltering. One of the plain-clothes detectives glanced her way, but it was the glance any man might turn towards an attractive girl.

They passed.

A woman close beside them said in undertones to the man with her: "What do you suppose those police are here for, honey?"

"I don't want to know," the man replied.

Ethel looked up at Mannering, and said in a low voice: "Do you think they've found him?"

"If they had I doubt if they would have let any passengers off the train," Mannering answered. "I wouldn't be surprised if they were there to pick up Ballas. If they've any grounds for holding him over the jewel robbery, this would be a good place." As Ethel's grip relaxed, he slid his arm under hers, and thrust her along towards a subterranean taxi stand. A small group of people were waiting, and several cabs drew up. No one took any notice of Mannering and Ethel. A youthful-looking coloured taxi-driver pulled up alongside them.

"The Conrad Hilton," Mannering said.

"Yes sir—that's the one on Michigan Avenue, I guess."

"Yes." Mannering helped Ethel inside, stood his suitcase on the floor, then climbed after her. No one followed them as they were driven past big, grey buildings, over big grey bridges, beneath a clattering roar of a train or tram going over a 'bridge' which stretched high above their heads in each direction.

"That's the elevated railway. We're in that Loop I was talking about," Mannering said, as if he were thoroughly familiar with Chicago. He glanced out of the rear window. "It's all right, Ethel. No one's following. Sit back and relax."

He expected her to echo, indignantly: "*Relax?* How could anyone?"

Instead, she shot him a sidelong glance, then stretched out her legs and allowed her body to sag. He saw how intently she observed the shop windows, the people on the sidewalks, the big taxis, the policemen. Soon, they were driving along a wide thoroughfare, with buildings on one side, parkland on the other. The taxi pulled up, a porter opened the door and took the bag.

"Have you a reservation, sir?"

"Yes."

"But —" Ethel began, but stopped abruptly.

"I'll bring your bag to the desk, sir."

"You can't let it out of your sight!" Ethel breathed into Mannering's ear.

"It's as safe with him as it will be with us," Mannering told her. "He won't get a tip if he loses it!" He led the way towards the right, through a throng of people all wearing little lapel badges. "Some sort of convention," he went on, glancing towards them, "and a pretty big one, too. It's a good job I booked!"

"You didn't book for me."

Mannering looked down at her, with a dry smile.

"There was a mistake. I booked for one, I should have booked for two."

"But —" Ethel began, but didn't finish.

They reached the desk.

"Have you a reservation, sir? . . . Mr. Mannering? . . .

A room for one person . . . *Two* persons, sir? The reservation said one . . . I'll see what I can do, sir . . . A twin bedded room or one bed . . . Twin-bedded, very well, sir . . . I doubt if we have one overlooking the lake . . . You specified lake-side? . . . It doesn't say so on the reservation slip but I will see what I can arrange, sir."

He disappeared behind a wooden partition.

"You know, if I hadn't heard so much about the Baron I might think you were a wolf," Ethel remarked without a change of tone.

"What does a child like you know about wolves?"

"Any child like me who doesn't know about wolves comes to grief very quickly," Ethel retorted.

"*Here* we are, sir, I've found one overlooking the lake, room Number 1515, I'm sure you'll like it."

Soon, they were standing by the window of Room 1515, and Ethel was looking out with an expression of plain disbelief, her eyes glistening, her lips parted. The vast lake, an inland sea which stretched far out of sight, lay shimmering in the morning sun. On a breakwater near them were half-a-dozen flags; inside the breakwater two or three hundred tiny boats bobbed. Between this window and the lake were wide thoroughfares dotted with cars, a railway line, bridges —

"It's magnificent," Ethel said, huskily. "I always thought Chicago was an *ugly* city."

"Only some of the things that happen in it," Mannering remarked.

That drew the light from her expression. She turned from the window, her eyes swerving away from the twin beds. She looked tired now, tired and very young.

There was a tap at the door, and Mannering called "come in." A porter appeared, with the case. When he had gone, Ethel stared at it without speaking, and Mannering took out a bunch of keys, unlocked, and threw back the lid.

Ethel's briefcase lay on the top. She could not look away from it.

"Ethel," said Mannering.

"Yes?"

"Why was Enrico Ballas so desperate to get that brief-case? He is a jewel thief, I've never heard he was involved in espionage."

She continued to look at it.

"I've never heard that my father was, either. *Nor* in jewels."

"The truth, please," Mannering insisted.

When she raised her eyes, her gaze was very direct.

"I have no idea at all why Ballas wanted that briefcase."

"He must have thought it very important."

"Obviously!"

"Did your father give you any hint at all about the cause of his alarm?"

"None."

Mannering locked the case and slipped the keys into his pocket. Sitting on the side of the nearer bed, he lifted the telephone. Ethel made no attempt to stop him or to protest, even when he said into the mouthpiece:

"I would like Whitehall 4–31495, please."

He held on, during odd noises on the telephone. Ethel moved so that her back was to the window. For one so young, she had remarkable poise and self-control. She knew he was about to speak to her father, her mind should surely be seething with anxiety and uncertainty, mused Mannering, yet she said nothing.

The bell went on ringing, the low-pitched note very different from the English *burr-burr! burr-burr!* Ethel's fingers began to clench, while Mannering asked himself what he could do next if her father did not answer.

He was on the point of hanging up when the ringing stopped, and a man said agitatedly :

"Ethel! Ethel! Is that you?"

"No, Professor Alundo," John Mannering said very carefully. "Ethel is with me, but before she speaks to —"

"She's all right? She *is*? Oh, thank God, thank God!" The voice rose suddenly. "You're not lying to me! This isn't some dreadful trick. *Please*. Is my daughter —"

"She's here, she's well, and she's not in any immediate danger," Mannering said. "Supposing you tell me why you think she is."

There was a pause. Ethel drew nearer, her eyes beseeching Mannering to allow her to speak, but he held her back with his free hand.

Then Professor Alundo said: "Has she got the notes? Has she got them? I must know—I must know whether she has them —"

He broke off abruptly, and Mannering had a sudden fear, that someone had come into the room and made the old man stop. He was aware of Ethel, watching with increasing tension; and he heard heavy breathing on the other end of the line. Then Alundo spoke in a calmer voice:

"Who *are* you? If you harm my daughter —"

"Your daughter will be all right once you've told me what you've done to make an enemy of Enrico Ballas."

The other man did not speak.

Ethel pressed closer and put out a hand to touch the telephone. Mannering did not let her take it, hardly knowing why he began to feel antagonism towards Alundo.

Ethel whispered: "Please let me speak to him."

"Before I tell you anything, I wish to speak to my daughter," Alundo said brusquely, and something of Mannering's hostility melted. "Kindly put her on the line."

Mannering relaxed his hold on the telephone. Ethel took it eagerly, seemed to take a very deep breath, and then said:

"Are you all right, Daddy?"

Mannering moved away, torn between waiting to hear

every word, in case any had special significance, and wanting the girl to have at least a sense of privacy. For a few minutes she talked reassuringly, and then her tone changed. She called:

"Mr. Mannering."

He looked round to see her covering the mouthpiece with one hand and looking at him.

"May I give Daddy your name?"

"Yes, of course."

She took her hand away.

"I'm with Mr. John Mannering, the antique dealer . . . Yes, Mannering . . . Well, *he's* heard of *you* . . . Yes, he's been a very great help . . . Yes, I do . . . Well, I *think* I can . . . Oh, Daddy!" There was exasperation in her voice. She listened for a long time, and then spoke quite sharply: "We haven't any choice . . . For goodness sake, can't you believe me?" During all this she was looking across at Mannering, and he was amused by her expression, as well as with the way she had lost patience with her father. Suddenly she burst out: "Oh, you're impossible, you really are! . . . Very well, *he* has the packet, I haven't, so we've *got* to trust him."

Mannering chuckled.

"And it's a good thing he's good-humoured about it. If it weren't for him heaven knows what would have happened to me." She listened for a few more minutes with obviously increasing annoyance, and then said in a tone of finality : "*I* can't promise that. You must speak to Mr. Mannering."

She thrust the telephone towards Mannering.

"He's *quite* impossible," she declared. "You'd better talk to him."

Mannering took the instrument and as he held it to his ear, Alundo was saying in a tone quite as sharp as his daughter's:

". . . you really must do as I say, Ethel. This is a matter

of extreme importance to me. Surely you have sufficient ingenuity to take it when he is not looking."

"Why don't you come and get it yourself?" suggested Mannering sweetly.

He heard Alundo catch his breath, and waited for an outpouring of apology. But none came.

"Mr. Mannering, that packet is mine. It is of value and of significance only to me. You have no right to it. If you are a man of integrity you will give it back to my daughter at once, and allow her to carry out my instructions. I insist that you waste no more time."

"I'm afraid it won't be so easy as that."

"If you want money," Alundo interrupted coldly, "I must inform you that I am a poor man. My daughter has to earn her own living."

"So I gathered," Mannering said. "I will be in the coffee shop of the Conrad Hilton Hotel at eleven o'clock exactly, with your daughter. If you want to see —"

"Mannering! That is impracticable. I cannot possibly be there! I have to be here, so as —"

"Where are you?" Mannering demanded.

"That—that is beside the point. Mr. Mannering, I *must* insist that you do as I say, and at once. Give the packet to my daughter, and let me talk to her. This is —" he hesitated, then went on as if inspired—"a very personal, indeed, a *family* matter."

"Professor Alundo," Mannering said, "Ethel and I are in Room 1515 at the Conrad Hilton, and will stay here for the next two hours."

He put the telephone down with enough noise for Alundo to hear. Ethel, only a little way from him, looked into his eyes.

"That's the only way to deal with him in these circumstances," she approved. "He really can be the most stubborn man alive. I'm sorry. Of course he doesn't know yet what you've done for me, but —" she shrugged—"well, even if he did he would be much the same. All he seems to care about is the packet of microfilm. What on earth can it be to make him behave like this?"

"Ethel," Mannering said quietly. "*Is* he a poor man?"

"Poor as a church mouse."

"Obviously this packet might be valuable."

"If you've got any idea that Daddy might be mixed up in something involving *money* you can forget it," Ethel said with utter conviction. "He might have some fantastic idea that he's saving the world from damnation or destruction, but you can certainly rule out financial gain."

"Unless he needs the almighty dollar to save the world," Mannering said dryly.

He watched her expression, and thought, quite unexpectedly, that this possibility had entered her mind before and that she didn't like it. She spun round towards the window and the shining lake, but Mannering had a feeling that she was no longer aware of the view, or the boats, or the traffic.

"Do you think he will telephone?" he asked her.

"I suppose he's bound to," Ethel said. "And I suppose all we can do is to wait. Unless —" she hesitated.

"Unless what?"

"You decide to let me have the packet, and I call him again and tell him I've got it."

"Not on your life," Mannering said with a chuckle. "Now that I'm involved, I'm going to stay involved. I want to know the reason, if any, for that coincidence."

"Then we'll wait," Ethel said.

They waited. Five minutes passed, then ten, then half-an-hour. Ethel sat in one of the two easy chairs overlooking the lake, her eyes closed but her lashes fluttering enough to betray her wakefulness. Mannering took a letter out of his pocket and began to read; it was in fact a summary of the details of the robbery at the Mayfair home of Lord Fentham,

and a close description, and history, of the Fentham diamonds. Only two pieces, a necklace and a bracelet, had been
stolen.

Mannering finished the letter, then glanced over some
pencilled notes he had made; the most significant stressing
the fact that the older Ballas, who lived here in Chicago,
possessed a superb collection of some of the finest diamonds
in the world. There was nothing at all surprising in any
attempt to steal the Fentham jewels for him, but there was
one mystery. The thief, or thieves, had stolen only two
items of the Fentham collection, when the whole or a very
much larger part of it could have been taken just as easily.
Why had Enrico Ballas—if it had been he—stolen only the
necklace and the bracelet?

Mannering studied photographs of the two pieces. The
gems were expertly graduated, the middle stones particularly fine specimens. Even in black and white they stirred
him; to Mannering there was fascination in beautiful jewels.

An hour slid by, and there was still no telephone call.

"He isn't going to ring," Ethel said. "He thinks he's got
more patience, and you'll ring him. I —"

She broke off abruptly, at a sharp tap at the door.

Almost on the instant, the telephone bell rang.

CHAPTER SEVEN

Visitor

AT Pennsylvania Station, Ethel had seen the bewildering speed with which Mannering could move, and now she had another demonstration. He seemed to sweep her to him with one arm and snatch up the telephone in the same movement. Into the telephone he said quite calmly : "Please call again later." To her, he said : "Stay behind the door. Don't move." He replaced the receiver and thrust her to a position in which she would be hidden when the door opened. All this, before there was another tap, even sharper.

"Just a minute !" Mannering flattened himself against the wall, opening the door while still standing on one side.

A man spoke in a voice so sing-song and unfamiliar that English ears could barely understand it.

"Waal, how *about* that?" The timbre of the voice seemed to swell in and out of the room, up and down the passage. "Did this door open by itself, d'you think? I'll be goddarned if it isn't enough to give me the heebie-jeebies."

In his most English accent, Mannering said:

"I can imagine that, sir. *Do* come in."

At the first sound of the stranger's voice, Ethel had started violently. Now she stared at the doorway in blank astonishment, as the door opened to admit their visitor, young, tall, good-looking in an angular, hawk-like way, wearing a wide brimmed Stetson and a pale beige-coloured suit of some smooth textured material which looked like mohair. He was so immaculate he did not seem real—nor did the gesture with which he thrust his hand at Mannering. "Good morning, sir. Do I have the pleasure of addressing Mr. John Mannering?"

"My name is Mannering."

"The *Baronial* Mr. Mannering? The dealer in antiques?"

"I deal in antiques," Mannering agreed.

The other man gripped his hand firmly.

"It is a great pleasure to meet you, sir, it surely is. It's one of the *great* pleasures." He gave Mannering a broad, warm smile, let his hand fall, and glanced round as if by chance. He saw Ethel. His eyes rounded, his lips dropped, he stared as if looking at an apparition, but before Ethel or Mannering could speak, he recovered, and went on : "Waal, how *about* that? Two great pleasures at one and the same time. Miss Ethel, it sure is a pleasure to meet you."

He stepped towards her, both hands outstretched, took hers and drew her very close to him; for a moment Mannering thought he was going to embrace her.

"I'll be goddarned," he went. "Your father certainly told me he had a beautiful daughter, but he didn't tell me you were *that* beautiful. Mr. Mannering, you be a witness, now. Isn't Ethel Alundo just about the prettiest young female you ever did set eyes on?"

"For goodness sake !" protested Ethel.

"Yes indeed," answered Mannering, beginning to enjoy himself, but still wary.

"You see?" The stranger drew Ethel even closer. "You wouldn't disbelieve a gentleman with such a reputation as the Baron Mannering, now would you, Honey? You certainly are the *prettiest* thing."

Ethel drew her head back, the only part of her she could move freely, and said in a clear, cold, carrying voice :

"And you certainly are the most ill-mannered person I have ever met. Please let me go."

He stared into her eyes, then dropped her hands as if they were hot coals.

"Miss Ethel," he said as if heartbroken, "I cain't tell you how sorry I am. I just cain't tell you. The last thing I would want to do to a beautiful woman like you is to cause any offence. I surely do apologise." He turned to Mannering. "Mr. Mannering, will you be good enough to bear witness to my apology."

Nothing in his expression or his tone of voice suggested that he was being facetious.

"I will," Mannering said. "If you'll tell me who you are and what you're doing here."

"Doing, sir?"

"Yes."

"But, the Professor —" The stranger broke off. "He promised to call you to say that he could not come and see you in person but had asked me to stop by instead. Didn't he call?"

At one and the same moment the telephone rang again. Mannering and Ethel glanced towards it; and the young man, seizing his opportunity to catch Mannering off guard, lunged forward, gripping Mannering's wrist and twisting him round so swiftly and savagely that pain shot through the arm from hand to shoulder. Mannering found himself held in a hammer-lock so tight that he could move neither to left nor right without danger of his arm being broken.

Ethel, who had swiftly snatched up the receiver, was saying: ". . . oh, all right, Daddy."

The young man spoke sharply into Mannering's ear: "You keep exactly where you are, Mr. Mannering, don't you try no tricks now."

The telephone gave an abrupt 'ting' as the girl rang off.

"Ethel," Mannering said, "don't trust this man. He's probably as dangerous as Ballas."

"Miss Ethel, you go pick up that packet your father wants, and you go wait for me in the lobby while I have an accommodation talk with Mr. Mannering."

"Ethel —" Mannering began.

"He *is* a messenger from my father," Ethel said in a low-pitched voice. "We'll have to give it to him." She moved, stepping into Mannering's sight—and in sight of his case, which was on a luggage stand. She tried to open it, but it was locked, so she turned to face him. "Where is the key?"

If Mannering refused to answer she would join the stranger in searching him, and there was no point in making that inevitable. With his free hand, he touched his hip pocket. Without a word, Ethel drew nearer, dipped her fingers inside, drew out his keys and turned away. Mannering watched as Ethel found the right key, opened the case, and lifted her own briefcase from the top.

"Is that it?" the young man asked eagerly.

"Yes, of course."

"Is the packet inside?"

She felt along the edge quickly, and said "Yes."

"Take it, Miss Ethel, and —"

"I'm not going to leave you here with Mr. Mannering," Ethel said in a very precise voice. "You take the case to my father, wherever he is. I owe too much to Mr. Mannering to let anything happen to him."

"But Miss Ethel, your poor father said —"

"Remind my father I am over twenty-one."

The grip on Mannering's arm did not slacken. He might break the lock, but it was probably better to pretend that he could not free himself. He sensed the tension between the two who were now both out of sight behind him. Before he could recover from his surprise at the girl's attitude, he was released, pushed heavily in the back and sent staggering forward, one arm outstretched to try to save himself from crashing into the wall. He did not see what happened but heard the thud of footsteps and the opening and the slamming of the door.

Mannering took more time than he really needed to

recover. It would be futile to rush after the young man, and would only make him look foolish. When he spoke to Ethel again he wanted to be in full command of himself, if not of the situation. So, he leaned heavily against the wall, flexing the muscles of the arm which had been held in that expert hammerlock. Then, slowly, he turned round.

Ethel was at the window, once again gazing out over the lake. The reflection of the sun on the water gilded her face and hair, making a breath-taking picture. Her head was high, her shoulders squared, her lips set. Even when she heard him approach she did not turn her head.

"There can't be another girl quite like you," Mannering said with quiet admiration.

That broke through her reserve, making her glance round.

"What do you mean?"

"I mean—thank you."

"Do you think I did the right thing?"

"I think you did what you thought ought to be done, in the best possible way."

She looked at him squarely.

"Mr. Mannering, I am very grateful for your help. When he knows what you did, my father will be, too. Now I think the best thing is for you to look after your own affairs."

"And leave you to look after yours?"

"I shall return to England."

"And wash your hands of your father?"

"I've done what he asked me to do."

Mannering studied the young, grave, troubled face, the grey eyes shadowed with thought. He needed no telling of the intensity of her feeling, or of her anxiety, and he felt a strange kind of compassion for her as he asked:

"Did he tell you to go straight back home?"

After a pause, she answered:

"Yes."

"And are you satisfied he can fend for himself?"

"I'm satisfied that he doesn't want help from me."

"As distinct from needing it?"

She drew in her breath, sharply, in annoyance.

"My father is a man of over sixty, and *quite* capable of making his own decisions."

"So having made his bed, he can now lie on it."

Ethel flushed.

"You are insufferably rude."

"And you are either being childish, or else you are very frightened."

Enunciating each word carefully, Ethel said: "Mr. Mannering, will you please leave me to look after my own affairs, and make my own judgements?"

"No, I will not," Mannering said. "In the first place, you and I have a mutual interest in the life and death of Enrico Ballas, and the police inquiries into his murder. We know he stole the microfilm from you—I believe he also stole some jewels from a client of mine. He may well have done both things for the same purpose—in which case your affairs are mixed up with mine and I don't trust your judgements. Don't interrupt!" he added sharply, as Ethel opened her mouth. "In the second place, whether you're frightened or not you have plenty of reason to be, and I don't want your life on my conscience. But I'll tell you what I *will* do."

She gave no sign of approval, but at least she was silent.

"I'll pretend to leave you on your own but keep an eye on you and see what happens. My guess is that Texas Tommy will be back for you soon—*he* won't want you to go home, even if your father does. You're much more likely than I am to find out if he's genuine."

Ethel looked troubled, but said nothing.

"Did your father say who his messenger was?"

Ethel hesitated. "He—he just told me to give him the packet and then to go home. Seriously," she added earnestly, "don't you think it would be better if I did go home, and you forgot all about this?"

"Nothing could make me," Mannering said. "Go down into the main lobby, Ethel. I'll bet T.T. will approach you within minutes."

"But if he took the packet to Daddy —"

"Try doing what I say," Mannering suggested.

Ethel moved to the dressing-table for her handbag, then to the door, opened it and said:

"I'm sorry if I behaved badly. I'm really very grateful."

Mannering smiled at her as she went out.

He waited for a moment, then locked the door on the inside, and turned to his suitcase; the key was still dangling from the lock. He opened it, lifted out the neatly folded clothes and accessories, until the case appeared to be empty. He pressed a fingernail against a spot in one corner, and there was a click—the unspringing of a metal fastener which held a false bottom into place. This gradually moved up the sides of the case, like overhead garage doors, leaving the secret space open.

Inside were Professor Alundo's lecture notes and the enclosed microfilm.

Mannering lifted them out, refastened the secret compartment, locked the case, then pushed the manuscript between his waistband and his shirt, so that it was secured by a leather belt. Covered by his jacket, the manuscript did not show.

He went out. No one was in the passage or in the lift waiting-hall. Down in the main lobby he saw Ethel looking in a shop window. He stopped a bellboy.

"Are there any lockers where I can check a parcel?"

"Yes, sir, downstairs in the arcade."

"Thanks." Mannering went down a wide flight of stairs, and came upon a row of metal lockers. He put a twenty-five cent piece into a slot at one of these, placed the manuscript inside, closed the door and took out the key. The door had locked automatically. No one appeared to take any notice of him. He made special note of the position of the locker, then went to a writing desk on the main lobby, wrapped the key in a sheet of paper and sealed it in an envelope, then took it to the main desk.

"Put this with the mail for guests who haven't arrived yet, will you?" He used a slow, drawling, American voice.

"Yes, sir. What name, please?"

"Mr. Mendelsohn," Mannering said. "It's a little gift for my wife—I don't want her to collect it when she comes for her key."

"I understand, sir."

Mannering waited for a few seconds, then moved away, satisfied no one had watched him; the mail "awaiting arrival" box was the last place where anyone would expect to find anything belonging to guests who had already registered. He sauntered back to the spot where he had seen Ethel.

She was still there—talking to Texas Tommy.

CHAPTER EIGHT

"*Texas Tommy*"

THE girl was arguing indignantly, and although the man kept his voice low, that remarkable intonation made a lot of people look round. They were arguing as young lovers might, Mannering reflected dryly. He walked past them, out of the side entrance, where there was a line of taxis. He approached the first driver and spoke in a drawling but natural-seeming voice.

"If I hire you for the day, will you do exactly what I tell you?"

A pair of deep-set, intelligent eyes studied him for a few second. Then:

"Sure. If it's legal."

"I want to find out where a Texan in a pale brown mohair suit and a ten-gallon hat goes," said Mannering. "I think he's a millionaire with designs on my daughter. If he comes out this way, you follow him, and I'll follow you." While speaking, Mannering took out a ten dollar bill and passed it over; it disappeared as if by sleight of hand. "If he uses the other entrance I'll come to the corner—you pick me up as fast as you can."

"You're taking a chance," the taxi driver said, and the bill hovered into sight again.

"I know." Mannering smiled, waving the money away. "Thanks." He went back into the hotel, seeing the Texan and Ethel still in the main lobby, but now the man's hand was on the girl's arm. Almost as soon as Mannering dodged behind a pillar, they began to move towards the entrance

c

from which he had just come. He turned and raced the other way, along Michigan Avenue and past bewildered passers-by.

When he reached the corner, the young man with the huge hat was moving off at the wheel of a Chrysler convertible. Ethel was beside him. The taxi driver was already following in their wake; as he caught sight of Mannering he winked. Ethel caught sight of Mannering, too, but her companion seemed interested only in the traffic ahead.

Mannering hailed another taxi.

This driver was as bright as the first, and soon caught up with him, staying a reasonable distance behind. They took two right turns, drove in the gloom beneath the elevated railway for several blocks, and then swung left along a wide street, jammed with traffic. There was nothing Mannering could do, so he sat back, relaxed, relying on the driver. Soon, they were among tall, red brick apartment buildings. Mannering saw the convertible turn into the driveway of a new block which seemed to be made of glass; both taxis passed, the leading one stopping two entrances along.

"Take the next right," Mannering said.

This was only fifty yards away, and soon, Mannering was speaking to the driver he had first hired.

"Leave my daughter to me," he ordered. "You keep track of Texas Tommy."

The driver grinned with friendly knowingness.

Mannering approached the new glass building, noting the sign outside which read :

LAKE VIEW APARTMENTS
$1\frac{1}{2}$: $2\frac{1}{2}$: $3\frac{1}{2}$: $4\frac{1}{2}$ ROOMS
APPLY: OFFICE IN LOBBY

The Chrysler convertible had been left in a parking space at the side of the forecourt. Mannering strolled past it, and saw a small, discreet sticker on the windscreen: FOUR SQUARE RENTALS. He was mildly surprised that this was a hire car. He turned in the direction of the main entrance, remembering idly the driver's amusement. None of this situation was really funny, but it had amusing overtones; the way the young man with the sing-song voice had behaved had been almost farcical.

But Enrico Ballas hadn't been farcical, in life or in death.

Nor was Professor Arthur Alundo.

Nor was the obvious danger to Ethel.

And Mannering found it difficult to believe there was anything funny about the microfilm. Why, he kept asking himself, should a specialist in jewels and *objets d'art*, switch to microfilm?—unless, of course, the film showed the mechanism of some safe or strong-room.

And why had he limited the Fentham theft to one necklace and bracelet? Until Mannering had found the answer to these questions, he would not, he knew, be at ease over this affair. But how could he find out more without questioning Alundo? And who in England would know if any important microfilm was missing; and whether Alundo was suspected, had ever been suspected, of spying.

In the cold light of what he already knew, this possibility did not seem ludicrous.

All of these thoughts flashed through Mannering's mind as he approached a doorman in a uniform resplendent enough for the Waldorf-Astoria.

"Can I help you, sir?"

"I think my daughter just came in," Mannering said easily. "I was to meet her here but I can't remember the number of the apartment. She was with a man in a pale brown mohair suit —"

"You mean they *just* came in, sir?"

"Two or three minutes ago."

"That was Mr. Ricardi, sir—with the blonde young lady."

"That would be her."

"Apartment 1701, sir—the seventeenth floor and turn right."

"Thank you," Mannering said, handing the man a dollar bill. "I'd like to surprise them."

He stepped into the elevator, pressed the button marked seventeen, and was taken up at a soundless speed; he was surprised when it stopped and the doors slid open.

He stepped into a wide, opulently furnished passage, coloured in blue and gold. As he did so, a man came out of a door three or four rooms along, on the right. He was tall and heavily built, and wore a tightly fitting suit, and under his left arm he carried Ethel Alundo's briefcase.

It was the man with the Irish look about him—the man Mannering had passed in the corridor of the Broadway Limited the night Enrico Ballas had been murdered.

Mannering stepped swiftly into an alcove, averting his face, but the Irishman passed without a glance in his direction, turning quickly into the elevator the other had just left. Mannering heard the doors slide to behind him. On that instant, he had a decision to make which was frightening in its possible importance.

He must either follow the man, or go to the apartment to find out what had happened there.

Texas Tommy—alias Ricardi—might simply have handed the briefcase over; or the big man might have been waiting, unsuspected.

He might be a knife-artist, too.

Mannering pressed the button of the second elevator, and heard a bell 'ding' almost at once. There was no time to go to the apartment; the doors slid open and he stepped inside, the elevator sinking swiftly to the lobby floor. The door-man was loitering in the hall, but there was no sign of anyone else. Seeing a notice marked CAR PARK AND

GARAGE, Mannering went towards it. He spotted his quarry at once, climbing into a green Chevrolet Impala, which stood near the Chrysler convertible in which Ethel and the young Westerner had arrived. Mannering leapt into the convertible—and saw his taxi driver sitting at the wheel just beyond the drive exit. He would understand a gesture to follow the Impala, but at this distance there was no way of warning him that the Irishman might be dangerous.

The man with the briefcase started his car and moved off.

Mannering, an expert with all locks and keys, was taking out his penknife which had a wire attachment—then noticed that the Westerner had been so preoccupied that he had forgotten to remove the ignition key. He started the Chrysler, stalled, started again, and went out slowly: the Impala turned right, and the driver was now out of earshot. The taxi driver put his head out of the window; that was the first time Mannering had noticed that he was cross-eyed.

"Okay?"

"The man in the Impala could be a killer."

"So he could."

"Can you find out where he goes, without getting involved?"

The taxi driver was already sliding forward.

"For how much?"

"Fifty dollars."

"Five hundred to my wife if I don't come back." The man grinned, as if he could wring a wry amusement even from the thought of disaster. His tyres squealed as he moved off. Mannering turned back into the driveway, watched by the bewildered doorman.

"Park the car for me," Mannering said, as he jumped out and hurried to the elevators.

It was not until he reached the seventeenth floor and was re-approaching Apartment 1701 that he began to feel really apprehensive. Until then, events had moved at a speed which had prevented anything but reaction; constructive thought had been impossible.

Now he began to fear what he might find inside the apartment.

He pressed the bell, but there was no response; when he pressed again there was still no sound of movement.

A strange change came over John Mannering in the few moments that he stood waiting; a kind of metamorphosis. It was a change that had come over him before, and would again—a change always the same and always of brief duration—one with which he was well familiar, even though he did not, at the time, realise it was taking place.

Many half-forgotten years ago, he had been an embittered man with a particular hate against society, and this hatred had turned him into a jewel-thief whom the world had come to know as "The Baron". Gradually, he had found that the excitement of breaking into the houses of the wealthy had become more important to him than his hatred; as gradually, he had found himself robbing the rich to help the poor, and others who had been ostracised or victimised by society.

In those days he had learned the secrets of a burglar's trade; of disguising his face, his body, even his voice.

It was all so long ago; yet it was this that had led him to the love of jewels, of antiques, of *objets d'art*, that was now part of his life. And his business, at Quinns in London, Boston, Paris and New York, had really been built on all he had learned as the Baron.

This lock should not give him too much trouble . . .

No conscious thought of the old days entered his head, as he bent over the door of Apartment 1701; only fear of what he might find inside. He took out the knife which had many blades and small tools—a set of tools, in fact, which would have made any policeman suspicious.

It looked like a straightforward Yale lock, and he selected one of the blades—a strip of strong mica which would gradually work through the key-hole, forcing the lock back once the pressure on each side was equal—and began to use it. Pushing it through seemed to take an age, and his heart was in his mouth when at last the lock clicked back. But nothing either slowed down or hastened the speed of his movements. He opened the door a few inches, stepped to one side, and called:

"Ethel!"

There was no answer.

"Ethel!"

There was still no answer, no sound.

Mannering pushed the door wide open and stepped inside—then stopped in the grip of dread. For three people were in this lovely sitting-room of reds and blues and subtle greens, of beautiful furniture and luxurious carpets. Three people, all inert; two sitting, and one, Texas Tommy, half lying on a long, low couch, face downwards.

Ethel Alundo lay back in a small chair, her face pale, her lips parted. A man obviously in his sixties sat, hunched, in a larger chair. He had a lot of untidy grey hair, a fresh complexion, a very lined face.

Not one moved, nor seemed to breathe.

At least there was no sign of blood.

Mannering went first to Ethel. He stared at her lips, and thought he saw a faint sign of movement. He lifted her left hand; her pulse was beating, though faintly, and he felt a surge of relief. Turning from the girl, he bent hurriedly over each of the two men, making sure they too were still alive— then he lifted the younger one more comfortably on to the couch. As he released him, he grunted; Texas Tommy weighed all of thirteen stone, in spite of his leanness. Mannering straightened him out, then stood back to assess the situation.

Knockout drops, he thought to himself, but which variety? On this would depend how long the three would remain unconscious. He examined the girl again, and found the tiny red mark of a puncture on her upper arm. Mannering knew that even a pin or needle-point smeared with pentathol could bring unconsciousness very quickly, and he did not try to picture what had happened here; he would find out soon enough.

Moving quickly past the inert bodies, he opened a door at the far end of the room, and found himself in a small passage. He stepped cautiously into the first room he came to, then stopped short, startled. This was not a bedroom as he had expected, but an office—and an unusual office at that. The whole of one wall was covered with enormous black and white aerial photographs, one showing a whole city spread out, with a section outlined by a wide white border. Over this section, composed of old houses, a few big buildings and a meandering river, was printed the word HEMIS-FAIR NINETY-TWO ACRES. Next to this photograph, on the same wall, was another, obviously an enlargement of the outlined section, yet totally unlike it. Here was a lay-out of an enormous exhibition, and written across or beneath most buildings were single word captions.

At the far end of the room, with just space enough to walk round it, was a table with a model, obviously to scale, showing exactly what the exhibition would look like; and preoccupied though he was with his own and the Alundos' situation, this caught and held Mannering's attention. He looked for JEWEL HOUSE, and found it leading off a big hall marked FOLKLORE SECTION. He half-smiled, but soon began to frown.

Why *had* Enrico Ballas been interested only in the Fentham necklace and bracelet? *Why* take only those and not the rest of the collection, which was worth at least as much again? And why did a jewel thief suddenly develop an interest in microfilm?

"The quicker I see what the film's about the better," Mannering mused.

There simply hadn't been time to investigate, but he must take time.

He cast a last, lingering look towards HEMISFAIR NINETY-TWO ACRES, then opened the door of the next room. This was a bedroom, and from the lecture notes and letters strewn about, it was obviously Alundo's. On a table near the bed were two telephones, one an extension of the Whitehall number.

Mannering retraced his steps along the passage, and listened for a moment at the door leading to the front room. But he heard nothing—its three occupants had obviously not yet recovered consciousness. Hurrying back to Alundo's bedroom, he picked up the telephone and put in a personto-person call to Chief Superintendent William Bristow, of London's Criminal Investigation Department at New Scotland Yard. The overseas operator told him there would be a twenty-minute delay. He replaced the receiver, then began a detailed search of each of the remaining rooms. One large main bedroom—with a luxury bathroom in pale blues and greens—was obviously Ricardi's, for four suits, each in its way as Beau Brummelish as the first, hung in a built-in wardrobe; a dinner-jacket was of powder blue. All the accessories, such as hair brushes, combs and toilet containers, were flamboyantly designed and exceedingly expensive.

In this room was a pile of beautifully prepared brochures about the HEMISFAIR, and another pile marked: GRAND OPENING—APRIL 6th. Mannering slipped one of each into his wallet.

There was no sign of woman's clothing—and no indication that anyone but Alundo and Ricardi were staying in the apartment.

Mannering found nothing to associate Ricardi with Alundo; only with wealth.

He went back to the sitting-room; no one had stirred.

He was used now to the eeriness of being with three unconscious people, and returned, once again, to Alundo's bedroom. The one spare suit was of poor quality, the oddments were all mass-produced and popular-priced. There was a travelling sample case which had been converted to a kind of travelling office, and in this were copies of the lecture itinerary, which had been arranged by the National Lecture Agency, with an address on 43rd Street, New York. Mannering tucked one of the copies into his pocket. He went through everything else in the case, but found little except letters about the lectures—praising, admiring, none of them critical. There was also a batch of correspondence about Alundo's forthcoming Peace Lecture, one of a programme of weekly lectures to be delivered in a place called the Convention Centre. Some of the most distinguished names in the philosophical and political world were here; Alundo was in excellent company.

Mannering closed the sample case, then turned to two shabby suitcases, but once again he found nothing of especial interest. And now the only thing unexamined was a battered brown leather briefcase.

This was locked.

He forced the lock without difficulty and opened the case with care. It was filled with neatly tied bundles of letters and telegrams, and two packets of press cuttings. He slid out two letters, and read furious attacks on Alundo—as a Communist, as a peace-at-any-price advocate; several more letters were in the same strain. The first three telegrams Mannering read were abusive; the fourth obscene.

At a rough calculation there were a hundred letters, fifty or so telegrams, and as many press cuttings. A typical headline of these read :

SEND THIS BRITISH RED HOME!

Mannering felt almost as concerned as if the attacks had been made on himself; yet running through this concern was a crack of doubt. *Could* there be anything in the accusations? *Was* he wrong about this innocent-seeming old man?

As he stood pondering, he heard a faint sound, the first he had noticed in the apartment. He moved swiftly but silently towards the partly open door, and glanced cautiously along the passage without revealing himself.

Professor Alundo was approaching, stealthily. In his right hand was an automatic pistol, on his lined face an expression of grim determination.

He was alone.

CHAPTER NINE

Alundo's Anger

MANNERING did not open the door wider, but moved to one side of the room, looking about until he found a spot where he could watch Alundo in the mirror. He dropped easily into a chair, positioning himself so that he could see without having to twist round, or be at a physical tension.

The older man seemed a long time coming.

Mannering found a confusion of thoughts passing through his mind. Even about this, there was a near-comic quality; the grim determination on Alundo's face was almost funny. Yet the situation might be graver than he yet knew; that microfilm could be carrying important secret information. Or was he letting his imagination run away with him?

Why was Alundo taking so long?

Mannering could hear his laboured breathing. He sat quite still, waiting expectantly while he wondered whether it was possible that Alundo would simply step round the door, and shoot.

The door moved slightly and a moment later Alundo's right hand appeared, the gun in it; then the side of a peering face. Mannering, watching the forefinger on the trigger, was prepared, at the slightest significant movement, to fling himself forward.

Alundo came farther inside the room, and Mannering saw that his hand was shaky. So was his voice:

"Stay—stay where you are!" he ordered shrilly.

Mannering stared as if taken by surprise.

"Stay there!" Alundo cried. "Don't move, or I'll shoot!"

Mannering felt fairly sure that even if he did, he was unlikely to score a hit.

"Who *are* you?" Alundo demanded.

Mannering said, quietly : "Professor Alundo?"

"Never mind who *I* am; I want to know who *you* are."

"John Mannering," Mannering said, and began to move.

"Stay where you are !" Alundo cried.

Mannering said : "If it weren't for me, your daughter would probably be dead. Put that gun away, and let's talk."

"How do I know you're not working for *them*?"

"For whom?"

"You know."

"I don't know what you're talking about," Mannering said, and paused. "I'm now going to get up. If you touch off that trigger, you'll have a murder on your conscience." He placed his hands firmly on the arms of the chair and began to rise. Every second seemed agelong, but at last Mannering was standing upright, facing the old man and the quaking gun.

"Don't come any nearer," Alundo warned.

"Don't you want to catch the man who robbed you?"

"How do you know I was robbed?"

"Because Ethel brought the briefcase to you, and when I arrived, I saw a man leaving with the case under his arm."

Alundo's eyes were bright behind his dark horn-rimmed glasses.

"Why didn't you stop him?"

"I had to find out what had happened in here."

"But it's more important to get that package back."

"Is it? Why?"

"Never mind *why*. It *is*."

"But I do mind why," Mannering said. "That's what's brought me here. What is the secret of those notes? What have you been up to?" As he spoke he moved slowly,

casually, nearing the old man, studying him closely. Several
things surprised him about the lined face—the well-shaped
lips, for instance, feminine lips, very like Ethel's; and the
startlingly blue eyes, the beautifully soft silvery hair. There
was something curiously winsome about him; it was as if a
Michelangelo cherub had suddenly grown old.

"Don't come any nearer," Alundo repeated, nervously.
"I don't want to shoot anyone —"

"If you shoot me you won't have a chance of getting the
microfilm back," Mannering said.

"What do you mean? That man has it."

Mannering said : "I mean what I say." He was almost
within reach of the gun, and could snatch or knock it from
the Professor's hand, without risk. But if he simply ignored
it he would not injure Alundo's pride so much, and he was
coming to believe that pride played an important part in
this man's life. "I mean that you are quite helpless against
these people, but I am not."

"*Why* aren't you?" demanded Alundo. "If you're not a
criminal —"

"Oh, don't talk nonsense," Mannering said sharply.
"What happened? How did he put all three of you out?"

Alundo lowered the gun, as if he had forgotten that it
was in his hand.

"I don't know," he said helplessly. "I was here on my
own, waiting for Ricardi and Ethel, and there was a knock
at the door. This man said he was from the Lecture Agency,
so I let him in. When he was inside he told me he had come
for the—the microfilm. When I told him it wasn't here, he
called me a liar. I'm not a brave man, and I freely admit
he frightened the life out of me! He asked me where the
film was, so I told him I was expecting Ethel and Ricardi to
bring it. He—he stuck a needle into my arm. I can remember feeling the numbness before I lost consciousness." Alundo
was speaking very quickly, as if he were still afraid. "I came

round just now and saw the others, and—I heard someone in here. That's all I can tell you." He flung the statement out almost defiantly, as if defying Mannering to disbelieve him.

Mannering asked: "Do you know who he was?"

"No."

"Do you know that his accomplice—or a man I believe to be his accomplice—was murdered on the train from New York last night? What is in that film to make men commit murder?"

Alundo remained silent; but he looked appalled.

"What is in that film? You must tell me, Professor."

"I *must*?" The blue eyes flashed with sudden anger, the well-shaped mouth tightened. "Who are you to tell me what I must tell you?" Alundo raised the gun, but his finger was not on the trigger. "*I* will be the judge of my behaviour, *I* will decide what I shall do. And I shall *not* tell you what is in the microfilm." The barrel of the gun actually touched Mannering's chest. "Please don't ask me again, because I mean what I say."

Mannering backed to a more comfortable distance.

"I'm sure you always mean what you say—but I don't think you're always right."

"I don't give a damn what you think. Every man has the right to think for himself. If he *can*, that is," Alundo added icily. "If he *can*. My goodness, if only people could think instead of react—if only they used their minds instead of their reflexes, if only they used their heads instead of their hearts. That's what we need, Mannering—people who can think for themselves, who don't have their thinking done for them. Now you're an intelligent man," he added simply, his burst of rage subsiding as quickly as it had arisen. "Do *you* accept this lunatic contention that war will settle anything? Tell me, *do* you?" He peered anxiously into Mannering's eyes. "Do *you* think war, violence, weapons, enmity, hatred—any of these things—will help humanity's problems?"

He paused for breath, allowing just enough time for Mannering to say:

"No, but apparently you do."

Alundo appeared not to hear him.

"Because they won't. The first thing this world needs is the outlaw of war and violence. Once that's done, once men realise there is nothing to be gained by fighting and hating, *then* we'll be on the way to understanding between peoples—*peoples*, I said." He waved the gun again, more vigorously, and his voice rose: "I mean *peoples*, not people. People understand each other. The man and woman who meet in the street, on trains, on buses, on tubes, in the theatre— *they* don't hate, they don't want to fight. But peoples, *en masse*— they are the tools and the fools of governments, of those imbecile, moronic, self-seeking, power-lusting maniacs who rule nations. *Peoples* can be made to do anything—hate, fight, rape, rob —"

He broke off.

Mannering said, off-handedly : "If there's one thing I can't stand, it's a man who doesn't practise what he preaches."

Alundo stared at him, aghast.

"Are you suggesting *I* don't practise what I preach?"

"That gun in your hand is a weapon," Mannering said, coldly.

"Gun?" Alundo, startled, glanced down, saw the pistol, raised it, then laid it on a small table. He threw out his hands. "But I wouldn't have shot you."

"How was I to know that?"

"You have my word for it."

"Professor Alundo," Mannering said gently, "don't you think that is one of the world's greatest problems—that people and peoples, politicians and governments, use weapons to frighten, and the frightened people then use other weapons to defend themselves against an attack which was never meant to be anything more than a threat. And that is what leads to war."

Alundo frowned, moved, dropped into a chair, crossed his legs, interlocked his fingers, and said :

'These are dialectics."

"You would have scared some people out of their wits with that gun."

"Don't you think *I* was frightened?"

"Yes," Mannering said, judicially. "But frightened people are dangerous. I think perhaps you are frightened too often and too easily. And now —" He paused. "What is in that microfilm?"

Alundo's mouth set obstinately, and Mannering was trying to decide what to say and do next, when the telephone bell rang.

He thought : "That's my call to Scotland Yard."

Alundo glanced impatiently at the telephone, as if willing it to stop. It rang with an impression of great urgency. Mannering moved towards it, glanced down and spoke as he lifted the receiver.

"This is Whitehall 4–31495."

"Mr. John Mannering?"

"Yes."

"This is the international operator. Your call to London is about to come through, Mr. Mannering."

"Thank you." Mannering looked across at Alundo, wondering whether to try to get the man out of the room, and then decided not to. "Shall I hold on?"

"Surely."

Mannering looked at Alundo, who began to get to his feet.

"It's for you, I suppose. Shall I leave —?"

"It's a call from Scotland Yard," Mannering said. "I'd

like you to hear what I say." There were a few odd noises on the line, and then he heard the voice of Superintendent William Bristow, once an enemy, now an old and trusted friend.

"Did I hear aright? That's John Mannering?"

"You heard me, Bill."

"You sound as if you're in the next room."

"I want you to hear me loud and clear. Bill—do you know anything about Professor Arthur Alundo?"

"Alundo? The self-styled peacemaker?"

"That's the man."

"I know he's a crank," Bristow said, and added quite unexpectedly : "He often seems to me to talk a lot of good sense, though."

Alundo was standing, now, too taken aback to protest.

"Do you know anything else about him?"

"Such as?"

"Is he a Communist?"

"Really!" exploded Alundo.

"He's got some red-tinged friends, but I don't think he's one himself."

"Is he a security risk?" asked Mannering.

"I must insist —"

"Not as far as I know," answered Bristow, and then added suspiciously : "Until a few seconds ago, it wouldn't have occurred to me."

"Do you think Alundo might know Enrico Ballas or his uncle?"

"Good God, no!" exploded Bristow. "What on earth makes you think he might?"

"A remarkable coincidence," said Mannering dryly. "Ballas was interested in the Professor and I'd like to find out why."

"*I* can't tell you," Bristow stated. "What's on, John?"

"I think Alundo may be in trouble over here."

"Mr. Mannering, will you please —"

"What kind of trouble?" asked Bristow.

"I don't know, except that Ballas tried to rob him, and someone else has succeeded. Ballas was only interested in jewels, wasn't he?"

Bristow said : "Old man Ballas has the most fantastic collection of jewellery and antiques outside a museum, and you know it. He got most of it by theft, and his nephew was one of the cleverest thieves in the business. John —"

"Yes?"

"What do you know about the nephew's death?" demanded Bristow.

"So you heard about that?"

"He'd just been to England, and the *Chicago Daily News* called our *Globe* and the *Globe* rang us." Bristow was silent for a moment, and when he went on he sounded very grave: "I should have connected a call from Chicago with the murder, but I didn't. Did *you* have anything to do with it Mannering?"

"No. I knew it happened, though."

"John," Bristow said with an earnestness which came very clearly over the telephone, "don't make any mistake about this. You're on your own. You can't expect any help from the Yard if you get yourself into trouble in Chicago. And the *Globe* took pleasure in reminding me that Enrico Ballas was one of his uncle's highly organised and very dangerous gang of international thieves. They are utterly amoral and unscrupulous, and if there was enough in it for them they'd probably sell out all the country's secrets. I haven't often heard the editor of the *Gobe* excited, but he was excited over this. If you've got yourself involved you could be between two fires—very dangerous fires. Are the police after you?"

"No," Mannering said, heavily.

"Come back to England before they are," advised Bristow.

CHAPTER TEN

Two Fires

WILLIAM BRISTOW would not talk like this for the sake of it; he was really worried.

Mannering, while listening intently to the Superintendent's words, was, at the same time, acutely aware of the indignation, the anger and even the distress on Alundo's face. The man stood only a foot or two away, one hand outstretched, as if to wrench the receiver from Mannering's grasp. There was no sound from outside, no sound in the room except their breathing.

Bristow asked, heavily : "Did you hear me?"

"Yes, Bill," Mannering said. "You advised me to come back to England while I'm safe. But there's something you've forgotten."

"What's that?"

"Not what. Who. Professor Arthur Alundo."

"Where does he come into this?"

"Mannering," Alundo called in an urgent whisper, *"if you tell him anything about me, I* will *shoot you!"* He moved surprisingly quickly as he spoke, and snatched the gun from the table. As he pointed it at Mannering, his hand seemed very steady, and there was open menace in his expression.

Mannering's whole body went tense, partly from the sudden danger, partly from this change in the old man; a few minutes before, he had dropped the gun as if in horror.

"Are you still there?" An urgent note came into Bristow's voice.

"Sorry, Bill, there was an interruption. Alundo doesn't come into this very much yet, but he's made himself some enemies."

"Including Ballas, you say."

"Yes."

"The Ballas gang doesn't do anything without a good reason. If Alundo is in any danger, make him go to the police," Bristow urged. "If you become involved in any crime over there, you'll be a bloody fool."

"You could be right," Mannering agreed. "If you get any news about Ballas's activities, let me know, will you? — care of the Conrad Hilton Hotel, Chicago. Thanks, Bill. Goodbye for now."

As he put the receiver down, Alundo replaced the gun on the table.

"I—I'm sorry about that," he muttered. "I don't *like* using threats, but —"

"You'll make them if they keep getting you what you want," Mannering said coolly. "I'd like to know whether you're a knave, a fool, or a hypocrite." He moved past the old man, picked up the gun, and slipped it into his pocket. "At least you won't be able to get at that again."

"Knave! Fool! Hypocrite! *Me?*" Alundo's voice rose.

Mannering looked him boldly in the eyes and said: "Yes."

Somehow, he felt it was a moment of truth and of testing. The old man's gaze was as direct as his, and for a few seconds they seemed as if they were playing the childhood game of staring each other out. Hostility was bright in those clear eyes; and accusation as clear in Mannering's. But even as they stared at each other, Mannering could not make up his mind what he really did believe.

A sound in the passage broke the tension.

Mannering could see the door beyond the other's shoulder, and once again he saw it slowly opening. He found himself gripping the gun inside his pocket—until he saw the pink varnish on the fingernails which appeared at the door.

"All right, Ethel," he said.

"Ethel!" Alundo spun round.

The girl came in, looking tired and pale but very relieved. Almost at once, there was a call as of alarm from the sitting-room, followed by heavy movements. A moment later, Ricardi came into sight, his hair rumpled, his jacket creased; he looked as if he had just woken up.

"What—what's going *on* here?" he demanded. Then: "I'll be goddamned if it ain't Mr. Mannering!"

Alundo was fussing over his daughter, showing more solicitude than Mannering had expected. Ricardi came fully into the room, and suddenly Ethel said crossly :

"Oh, Daddy, for heaven's sake!" She eyed Mannering very steadily. "I suppose you'll gloat, now. The briefcase was stolen from us as soon as we got here, we would have been wiser to leave it with you. We had hardly got inside the flat," she added, bitterly angry with herself. "A man was waiting just inside the door. He snatched the case, jabbed a needle into me —"

"And into *me*, by golly!" Ricardi put in.

"If you'd had your wits about you, you would have stopped him," Ethel said scathingly. "Well—we might as well give up, I suppose."

"Give up?" echoed her father. "You're out of your senses. We've got to get that film back."

"We certainly have to do just that," Ricardi said. "Baron Mannering, sir, I have been hearing plenty about you, I certainly have, and according to Ethel here you're a big-shot detective. Will you find that microfilm if I pay you a mighty big fee in advance? Say, ten thousand dollars?"

Mannering did not speak, but was acutely aware that all three were staring at him expectantly. When he did not answer, Ricardi said eagerly :

"So ten thousand isn't enough. Will you settle for *twenty* thousand?"

If he were serious, and all the indications suggested that he was, then the microfilm was worth at least twenty thousand dollars to him. The realisation startled Mannering. What could the film contain to make it worth so fantastic a sum?

More slowly, Ricardi said: "Twenty-*five*."

"Mannering —" began Alundo.

"You can't possibly afford —" Ethel began.

"Don't worry about what I can afford," said Ricardi. Quite suddenly he seemed more mature and completely sure of himself. "I've a hundred thousand acres of Texas range, and a steer on every ten acres on top of it. Underneath that, I've got the oil. You don't have to worry about dollars, honey."

Mannering thought: I really believe him.

Ethel looked dumbfounded.

Then Mannering wondered: If he isn't in this for the money, what *is* that microfilm about?

Before he could hope to make any progress, he must have time to think; meanwhile he must appear to be persuaded by the size of the fee. Then he recalled his own reputation, and suddenly made up his mind what to do.

"Is it a deal, Mannering?" Ricardi demanded.

"Ten thousand dollars," Mannering said, "with another ten if I find the film."

"There's no 'if' about it!" cried Alundo. "That film *must* be found."

"Mr. Mannering," Ricardi said, stepping forward with his hand outstretched. "You're a gentleman."

He had a cool, firm hand.

"When are you going to start? Do you know the thief? Where —" began Alundo.

"Daddy," interrupted Ethel, exasperatedly, "sometimes I think you will *never* grow up."

"I know where I might find the man who took the brief-case," Mannering said. "I'll be back in an hour, and I'll want to know all you can tell me—where you got the microfilm, why it's worth so much to a Texan millionaire, when the attempts to steal it began, and —" he moved across to the battered briefcase whose lock he had forced, opened it, picked up one of the bundles of abusive letters and held it out—"when these letters started to come, and whether the telephoned threats on your life were because you preach peace-at-any-price or because you had the micro-film."

He put the bundle of letters in Alundo's hands, and went through the door, closing it carefully behind him.

Outside, he paused and listened, but none of the others spoke, and none seemed to move. He walked slowly along the passage, paused again, but was not followed. Stepping into Ricardi's bedroom, he opened the sliding door of a wardrobe; it was filled with clothes, including two jackets rich in colour and extravagance. He slipped into one and then found a linen cap, in wine red. Putting this on care-fully, he hurried to the sitting-room, opened the main apart-ment door cautiously, and peered outside. No one was in sight. Nevertheless, he felt on edge as he waited for the ele-vator, which whined softly on its way up. The door slid open, and he stepped inside. He felt increasing uneasiness, as if his warning antennae were picking up danger signals; it might be because of what had happened here, it might be because of what Bristow had said.

No one was in the main lobby.

Still cautiously, Mannering reached the street doors—and started with alarm when he saw the doorman in deep con-versation with one of the detectives who had been at the railway station. The doorman was talking with great earnest-ness. Mannering looked round and saw a telephone under a hood on the wall. He stepped to this, put in a ten cent piece, and began to dial Whitehall 4–31495. As the ringing echoed in his ear, footsteps sounded in the lobby.

"Sure, he was a big guy," the doorman was saying. "Said she was his daughter." The voices faded as the men reached the elevator.

Why didn't someone answer?

Almost on that instant, Ethel answered: "Hallo?"

"Ethel," Mannering said, "the police are on their way up. I think they want to talk to you and to me. You mustn't know anything about the murder on the train—just say you don't know a thing about it."

He rang off without waiting for her reply, went to the side entrance, wondering how many police would be there, saw none, walked towards the front, and recognised a plain-clothes man standing by the side of a car which was not marked POLICE. Just beyond this, in the roadway, was a taxi and at the wheel the driver who had followed the brief-case thief. He saw Mannering, but gave no sign of recognition; and Mannering felt a surge of relief. Ricardi's jacket and cap were standing him in good stead.

He walked boldly past the man in plain-clothes, who glanced at him incuriously, then turned out of the drive-way and towards the taxi. The driver seemed to be more interested in his clothes than his face. The driving window was down, and as he passed, Mannering startled the man by saying out of the corner of his mouth :

"Meet me round the next corner in five minutes."

The taxi man waited a moment, then started off.

Exactly five minutes later he pulled alongside Mannering and opened the rear door without a word.

"Seen a ghost?" demanded Mannering.

"Would never have recognised you," said the driver. His voice was subdued, it was obvious that something had disturbed him. "You want to talk here?"

"I'd rather go somewhere quieter."

"We'll go to Grant's Park," the taxi-man decided, obviously as anxious as Mannering to get away. "Near the Planetarium. Okay?"

"That will do very well."

"Mister," said the taxi driver, starting off, "you owe me five hundred bucks."

"What cost you the extra four-fifty?" Mannering asked.

Without turning his head as he moved into the flow of traffic, the other answered :

"An English gent like you would call it bloody scary."

"Scary," echoed Mannering, his tension rising. "What scared you?"

"Do you know who the big guy was?"

"No."

"Tiger O'Leary," said the taxi driver, and this time he turned his head, as if to judge Mannering's reaction. He gave the impression that he expected the name to have a sensational effect, but Mannering kept straightfaced, and asked:

"Should I know Tiger O'Leary?"

"He's the chief trouble-shooter for Mario Ballas."

"And should I know Mario Ballas?"

"You mean you've never heard of *him*?" The taxi-man whistled. "You really mean that?"

"You forget I'm an English gent," Mannering said mildly.

"But he's the biggest big-shot criminal in the world!"

"Or Chicago?"

"In the world, mister. He's the Mafia, plus plenty. He's the biggest." The man's voice was hoarse, and it was clear that he meant every word he said. His shoulders hunched over the wheel and in a strange way he looked older; even coping with the traffic seemed more difficult for him. A sleek red Thunderbird sped by, very close. They were on a road which threaded through parkland, sparsely wooded; on one side were the tall buildings and, beyond them, the down-town skyline; on the other were the highways, the open grassland and the lake. Traffic hummed.

Suddenly, the driver went on: "I tell you he's the worst."

"Why are you so sure?"

"That's the trouble, I don't know where to begin, mister. If you don't know — You read the newspapers?" he asked abruptly.

"Yes."

"You see the headlines about the murder on the Broadway Limited."

"Just the headlines," Mannering said.

"The stiff was Ballas's nephew, and that will make Mario mad. Real mad." The taxi driver drew in a sharp breath. "When he's mad, he'll be worse than ever. Mister —"

"Yes?"

"Did you cross Ballas up?"

"Yes," said Mannering calmly. "But I didn't know who he was."

"You know now. And you crossed him up. Make that a thousand bucks, mister."

"No man can be as bad as that," protested Mannering, but he began to feel cold.

"Some guys can be. Ballas *is*."

They were slowing down near a huge car park outside the dome of the Planetarium. The taxi driver pulled into an open space. Some children were playing noisily a few yards away, a young couple sat very close together in an old blue car, not far off. In the distance a few people walked, over the lake the sun shone with glittering brilliance, and here and there a white sail showed. The scene was peaceful, almost idyllic. The taxi driver stopped the engine with great deliberation, and turned round. Mannering, puzzled by his expression, actually wondered for a moment if it was the same man.

"If he's as bad as that, why are you here?" he asked.

"Mister," said the taxi driver, "I don't like guys like Ballas, no, sir, I don't like them. They still run protection rackets in Chi, and one of the rackets is in cabs. I'm an independent owner, and there aren't so many of us left— most of us were driven off the streets by Ballas or one of the other mobs. You following me?"

Mannering said quietly: "Very closely."

"I don't intend to get involved with Ballas," the taxi driver went ŏn. "But you're a stranger. So whatever you have on him today, forget it. Don't try to work on Mario Ballas. He's everything I've told you and more. You want some advice?"

"I'll listen," Mannering said.

"Get out of Chicago—quick."

Mannering said : "I might, at that."

"You'll be crazy if you don't," the driver said. "You'll be dead crazy." He gulped. "So don't say I haven't warned you. You want to walk?"

"Can you take me to State Street?"

"No, sir, I'm not taking you any place," the driver said. "You can get plenty of cabs over by the Planetarium, you won't have to walk." He leaned across and opened the door.

Mannering said : "Where does Ballas live?"

"He's got a place in Chi, and a place in Mexico."

"Whereabouts in Chicago?"

"You can ask someone else, mister."

Mannering shrugged.

"If that's how you feel." He took out his wallet, and extracted fifty dollars, two twenties and a ten, and handed them over the back of the seat. He noticed the police licence and photograph of the driver : Peter Gulack, No. 43124. The man took the bills and tucked them away.

"I'm sorry, mister," he said. "I've got to live."

Mannering nodded. Standing by the side of the taxi, he felt unexpectedly cold, despite the warmth of the sun. The children were laughing with carefree abandon. He tried to fight off a mood which was not far from depression as he set out at a brisk pace towards the road. Two or three taxis were pulling up outside the main entrance of the Planetarium. A notice board extolled the wonders of the skies. He hailed a taxi but it drove past, the driver covering the flag of the meter with his hand. Another passed, hailed by a middle-aged man. A third pulled up. Mannering got in, dropped heavily on to the back seat, and said:

"Marshal Fields, in State Street."

The driver grunted, and Mannering leaned back, watching the scene. The taxi was moving very fast but he took little notice until he realised they were swinging off the main highway. He was thrust against the side by the sway of the car, then sent lurching forward as the driver jammed on his brakes. On the instant he knew what had happened— he had allowed himself to be fooled by one of the oldest tricks of all, a stooge taxi. The road was narrow, running through rows of small trees, and before he could do more than realise his danger, the car jolted to a standstill. Almost at once, two men appeared. Slowly they began to close in, and when Mannering looked through the opposite window, he saw two men closing in on this side also.

Everything he had ever heard about Chicago gangsters screamed through his mind.

The taxi driver sat motionless, staring ahead.

"A thousand dollars if you drive straight on," Mannering said in a clear voice.

The man didn't answer.

"*Two* thousand."

The man muttered : "You're wasting your time. Tell them what they want to know."

Mannering saw sweat on the man's upper lip, and knew that he hated the situation almost as much as he did himself.

Almost ...

The four men were very close; each was powerful and thickset, and each looked menacing. One of them was Tiger O'Leary; Mannering did not think he had ever seen an uglier face.

CHAPTER ELEVEN

Mario Ballas

THE four men were now within a few feet of the taxi. The driver's breathing came in heavy, laboured gasps. He stared straight ahead. Mannering, very tense but curiously un-afraid, opened the nearside door, and climbed out. As he straightened up, the taxi engine snorted, the driver jammed his foot on the accelerator, and the cab shot off in a cloud of dust. Immediately the four men, adroit and deadly, surrounded Mannering, shutting off all possibility of escape.

O'Leary stood nearest to him.

Mannering said : "Good morning," firmly and clearly. No one could guess the speed at which his mind was working. If only he could find it in time, there must be a way to lessen the danger; perhaps even to turn the situation to his advantage.

O'Leary, an inch or two taller and much heavier than the others, banged into him, obviously by intent. Another man was at Mannering's other side, the shortest of the four, and the smallest. He had narrow, rather fine green-grey eyes and a well-cut mouth.

"Are you John Mannering?" this man asked. He almost said 'Man'ring', and his voice was hard but low-pitched.

"Yes," Mannering said pleasantly. "Are you from Mario Ballas?"

The speaker looked startled; one of his companions smothered an exclamation.

"What do you know about Mario Ballas?"

"Not enough," Mannering said.

"A goddamned sight too much," growled O'Leary. "Cyrus, you can't —"

"I'll do the talking," said the man named Cyrus, his glance unwavering.

A very slight feeling of relief touched Mannering. In those few critical seconds he had called on all his subconscious ingenuity for a tactical approach to turn the situation to advantage, and he believed he had found one; certainly the first reaction could be accounted good. It was a relief to find O'Leary rebuked; he seemed the most hostile. Mannering showed none of this relief, nor did he overdo the nonchalance. The remarkable thing was, that he still felt quite untroubled. He waited while Cyrus studied him, as if trying to make up his mind what to say next; and Mannering judged him to be a man not likely to be often in doubt.

"Did you put a knife into Enrico?" Cyrus asked at last.

"No," Mannering said.

"I hope that's the truth—for your own sake."

"I don't answer any question more than once," said Mannering shortly. "How soon can I see Mario Ballas?"

"What makes you think you can see him?"

Slowly, very deliberately, Mannering said : "Do you really believe he would approve of this waste of time?"

O'Leary rammed an elbow into Mannering's ribs, with intentional brutality, and Mannering wondered if he had goaded him too far. No one spoke, until Cyrus said:

"I don't waste time. Why do you want to see him?"

"I'll tell him that," Mannering said.

"Cyrus," O'Leary said with harsh, menacing certainty, "why not *make* the guy talk?"

This time, Mannering did not ignore the interruption but turned towards O'Leary and looked at him. A quiver of apprehension returned. O'Leary's bloodshot eyes were hot, glassy, lowering, and the ugly lips were brutally square.

Cyrus was human; O'Leary was nearer the savage. His jutting chin and big ears had an aggressive cut.

"I will talk only to Ballas," Mannering said. "It wouldn't take much to make me tell him I think you are a punk." They held each other's gaze for a full minute before O'Leary's wavered. Cyrus broke in, almost as if to pacify O'Leary.

"You'll do what you're told," he said harshly. "And the first thing is, you'll walk with me."

He half-turned, and Mannering joined him. The others followed, O'Leary very close behind. For the first time since he had got out of the car, Mannering was able to look about him. This was a secluded spot among trees, and no one else was within sight, although he could hear the distant hum of traffic and the faint shouts of children. He guessed that he was walking towards the main highway which led from the promontory on which the Planetarium was built. Two grey squirrels were leaping from branch to branch, the leaves rustling in a gentle wind.

The sinister little party of men broke through the trees to a clearing where two cars waited, the green Impala which Mannering had seen outside the apartment block, and a Ford station wagon. A man was standing by the side of each. Mannering walked easily, without glancing behind him, and O'Leary no longer touched him. Cyrus led the way to the Impala, and the man beside it opened the rear door. Mannering got in. O'Leary moved swiftly to the far side, to make sure he could not bound straight through the car and run for safety, but Mannering settled himself comfortably in one corner.

"Your friend doesn't seem to believe that I want to see Ballas," he remarked easily, as Cyrus got in beside him.

"Who said *I* believed you?" Cyrus demanded. "Don't get this the wrong way round, Mr. Mannering. Mario Ballas sent for *you*."

D

A smile hovered about Mannering's lips.

"Did he indeed?"

Leaning back in the car, he was aware of Cyrus's curious gaze, of the fact that he had them all puzzled. Then O'Leary took the seat next to the driver, and the car started off. Mannering, intent on memorising the route they took, peered out of the window, wondering where Mario Ballas lived, whether they would go straight to him, what the man would be like. He was reminding himself that Enrico Ballas had been murdered, and it now seemed as if Ballas as well as the police suspected him, when he felt a sharp, pricking pain on his hand. He jerked it upwards, turning towards Cyrus, and had time for a swift, alarming glimpse of a sardonic smile.

Then he began to lose consciousness.

When Mannering woke, he was alone.

He was lying full length on a narrow bed. The room was small, with a high window of thick, frosted glass. As consciousness came back, he looked about him. The furniture was old, and of carved oak—it had an un-English, more a Spanish look. In a corner was a decorated hand-basin, and some of the biggest brass taps, intricately shaped, he had ever seen. There was one door; it was opposite the window, and looked almost impregnable.

In five minutes or so, he felt quite clear-headed; whatever form of knockout drops they used had no after effects. Everything Ballas used would be good. And could be deadly. It was easy now to understand how the man could strike such terror into his fellow human beings. Getting off the bed, he went towards the hand-basin. Clean, snowy-white towels hung on the brass rail. He washed his hands and face, dried them and turned to the door much fresher and able to think swiftly. He tried the big, ornate brass handle, but the door was locked.

Near the hand-basin was a chair, and he pulled it to-wards the wall beneath the window; it was so heavy, he had to exert considerable strength. He climbed up on to the chair, not expecting to see anything through the frosted glass, but had a welcome surprise; two or three smooth patches showed a clear blue sky. He shifted his position and then saw land; he was so astounded that he nearly slipped off the chair.

Rocky, almost barren ground stretched to the horizon, which was broken by a range of mountains. He stared for what must have been several minutes, but nothing moved; *nothing*. The sun was vivid, burning the earth to a hard, grey surface.

They had flown him here, of course. But where was 'here'?

The question was hardly in his mind before he remembered the taxi driver telling him that Mario Ballas had a house in Chicago and another in Mexico.

This certainly wasn't Chicago—and the old oak furniture was almost certainly Mexican.

Slowly, he climbed down from the chair. He felt almost stupefied, for he must be a thousand, perhaps two thousand, miles from Chicago, and consequently, very much more helpless.

Trying not to think about this, he ran through his pockets and found everything in place, even the knife with the special blades. Men who worked for Ballas would know what that was for; so they had deliberately allowed him to keep the tools with which he might be able to force this lock.

Why? And—should he work on it?

He felt tired and badly shaken, depressed by the relent-lessness of the land beyond. He went back to the bed, trying to relax, trying to keep his mind blank. As always when this happened, he pictured his wife's face. Lorna's. He had not seen her for over two weeks, for she had gone to Scotland to paint the portrait of the twin sons of a Scottish laird; and while she had known of his proposed visit to the HemisFair in San Antonio, she knew nothing of his second purpose in coming to America. She had known of the theft of the Fentham jewels, had known that Lord Fentham had been sufficiently troubled over their loss to enlist Mannering's help, but was as yet unaware that it was the pursuit of these jewels that had led Mannering to New York.

Mannering could picture Freddie's face as well as Lorna's; a face of dignity and kindliness, a lover as well as a collector of *objets d'art* and precious stones, a man reputedly of illimitable wealth. Why should the loss of these particular pieces—both of which were doubtless insured—appear to trouble him so much? That question had been worrying Mannering since he had heard Fentham's story. Now, he could almost imagine the sound of his voice.

"John, you're the only man in the world who knows, but this loss is a very severe blow"—who could doubt how much he meant that?—"and you're the only man in the world who might be able to get them back for me."

Mannering had not wanted to be involved. Business at Quinns in London, New York, Paris and Boston was good, and kept him busy; these days he did less and less investigation into crimes, but for an old friend—and in view of his interest in the HemisFair in San Antonio . . .

Thought of that pulled him up with a start. Was Texas like the land beyond the window? West Texas, particularly —and the land near San Antonio? Texas and Mexico had a common border for hundreds of miles.

He forced his mind back to the missing diamonds.

Word had reached the manager of his Mayfair shop that Enrico Ballas was in London, and had been seen near Fentham's home. This kind of information seldom reached the police, but often reached Mannering. But for this, he wouldn't be here; but for Fentham, he wouldn't be here . . .

He could picture Lorna's wry smile, the hint of laughter in her grey eyes which touched her face with beauty.

"But for *you*, you wouldn't be there!"

If he had never been the Baron . . .

He half-laughed at himself, much as Lorna would have done, and sat up again. Now he felt almost normal, his eyes and head free from pain. He went to the door, deciding to force it; obviously this was what he was expected to do. Before taking out his knife, he tried the handle again.

The door opened.

Could it have jammed before?

He felt sure that it had not, that this was part of the tactics being used against him. He opened the door slowly and stepped into a dark passage, on to a floor of uneven oak, leading to a hall which was furnished in the same way as the bedroom. Stained glass at the doors and the adjoining windows, added more than a touch of gloom. Several unlighted oil paintings hung on the walls—one, at a cursory glance, could have been an El Greco, and in one corner Mannering noted a huge, carved cupboard, rich with the bloom of centuries of polish. The big, square carpet looked Persian, but might be Indian; it was impossible to tell in so dim a light. A wide, stone staircase led up to a half-landing, and above this was a gallery. Everywhere, Mannering had an impression of dull lustre, of richness.

The front door was on his right, facing the foot of the stairs. He saw no chains in position and no bolts were shot home. He tried the handle, and it turned without difficulty.

Could he have been left alone in an empty house?

He rejected the thought as it came to him. Tactics, he told himself, *tactics*. This was deliberate; they were virtually inviting him to run away. They would not let him get far, but obviously they were trying to prove something. What?

He thought he knew; they wanted *him* to prove that he

really meant to see Mario Ballas, even to the point of reject-ing a chance of escape.

He glanced over his shoulder. No one was in sight, nothing moved, there was no sound. Any dark corner, any doorway, might conceal a man—half-a-dozen men. He had the sense of being watched; of unseen but seeing eyes. He turned his back again and opened the door; he was almost afraid of being shot, but nothing happened. The door gave a sharp creak as it opened wide.

The flagged porch or patio stretched far to the right and the left. The house in which he was standing was one of four long, low buildings in Spanish style, which surrounded a paved courtyard, in the middle of which was a wrought-iron fountain. From cracks or gaps in the paving a variety of cacti grew, one a prickly pear, one like a yucca, one which looked almost like a sheep. Some of the cacti had branches or leaves, like broadswords. The sun beat fierce and vivid on to the courtyard.

No one appeared.

Mannering drew back into the shade, deliberating. He could not be sure but he was probably in an isolated spot, virtually in the middle of nowhere. He ventured into the courtyard, and found an old ladder, the rungs secured to the supports by leather thongs. He rested this against the nearest roof, and climbed up it. At the top, he had an un-interrupted view in all directions—but except for a huddle of tiny huts, he could see nothing but the barren, rocky land, across which an unsurfaced road ran out of sight. Nothing, that was, but three small aircraft beneath a raffia roof sup-ported by corner posts. He stared at them for a moment, then climbed down the ladder and walked back to the door through which he had just come. Seeing a big brass bell-push, he placed his finger on it. Somewhere a long way off he could hear the reverberation of sound. He rang for much longer than was necessary before he took his finger away.

At last some small noise caught his attention.

The man named Cyrus appeared from one of the rooms leading off the hall from which Mannering had previously emerged. The sunlight showed him alert and smiling.

"Good afternoon," said Mannering. "Does Mr. Mario Ballas live here?"

Cyrus's smile stayed, unaltered in expression.

"Come in," he said, and stood aside. As Mannering stepped over the threshold, a light came on above his head; more lights followed, and as the door closed behind him, hall, staircase and landing were all transformed. Cunningly placed spotlights shone on the paintings, revealing their beauty; Mannering could recognise a Rembrandt, a Gainsborough, a Titian. What he had thought to be a cupboard proved to be the reredos from some old church—a crucifixion scene, showing hundreds, perhaps a thousand, exquisitely carved figures, each one he looked at perfect in execution.

Mannering stood quite still, glancing about him.

"You needn't waste your professional acumen looking too closely," Cyrus said dryly. "All that you see has been bought on the open market. This way."

Mannering went ahead of him, up the stone staircase leading to the half-landing. The Persian runner here was of soft, warm colours; there were two Rubens and a Reynolds on the walls. Glancing up at the ceiling, Mannering saw a crucifixion mural worthy of any cathedral; it looked more modern than classical—possibly Mexican, he thought.

They reached the landing. Two men were stationed there, incongruous in their modern clothes. One of the men was standing, heavy and truculent, against a dark, solid-looking door. It was Tiger O'Leary. He moved aside with obvious reluctance as Cyrus brought Mannering towards him.

That taxi driver had certainly known what he was talking about.

"All right, Tiger," Cyrus said.

"I tell you you're crazy," O'Leary growled.

"Then Mario's crazy."

"If you ask me, you're *all* crazy."

Cyrus shrugged, and tapped at the door.

Mannering felt as if he were standing in a film set under the glare of cinema cameras, so unreal did the whole scene appear to him. Only O'Leary's heavy breathing and undisguised hostility gave the touch of real and pressing danger. They waited for a few moments, and then he heard a movement at the door. He sensed rather than saw a peephole open, heard it slide to. Another sound followed. Immediately, Cyrus turned the handle and pushed the door open. He went in first, and stood aside.

Mannering entered the room.

It was remarkable, not only for its size but for the fact that it was less a room in a private house than a church turned into a museum.

For the second time since he had recovered consciousness, Mannering stood astounded.

He had entered from the middle of one of the long sides. How long, he wondered? At least fifty feet both right and left. The walls looked like those of an ancient Spanish mission, uneven, plastered, patched. In innumerable niches, and on as many small shelves and brackets, were *objets d'art* from all four corners of the world.

Between these were paintings of so great a beauty that now the collection outside seemed almost trivial. At intervals were small windows, deeply recessed, showing the thickness of the walls; four feet at least. Above, were heavy beams, dovetailed in such a way that each appeared to form part of a cross; some were thrown into relief by spotlights illuminating carvings as beautiful as those on the reredos.

These things, by themselves, would have made this the most remarkable room which Mannering had ever seen—but the remarkability was heightened by the bizarre occasion of his seeing it, shanghaied and drugged as he had been, and guarded now by such a brute as Tiger O'Leary.

His first astonishment over, Mannering noticed with delight that every inch of space was crammed with *objets d'art*, antiques, paintings and sculptures; and that against the walls were show-cases, in which scintillated countless gems.

There was order of a kind in the arrangement; and gradually Mannering became aware of this. The centuries were gathered together—Byzantine, Egyptian and Babylonian, Grecian and Roman—through to the Middle Ages, the Rennaissance, and even to modern art, which was represented by a fantastic abstract; a Picasso, unless Mannering was mistaken, but one of which he had never heard.

At one end of the room was a desk, delicately inlaid with enamel; and behind the desk, a chair that was like a throne, composed entirely of bejewelled gold. From a narrow, brass-studded door a man entered. He did not glance towards Mannering or Cyrus, but went towards the chair, moving with the slow deliberate movements of the very old or infirm. He was small, and slightly built, dressed in a beautifully cut suit of black velvet, with short Spanish-type jacket and tight-fitting trousers. His shoes were traditionally those of a bygone Spain. His eyes were hooded, his features a little too smooth and regular. Noting this, and the brilliance of his eyes and lips, it occurred to Mannering in a macabre flash of prevision that he was like a corpse, made up for the last respects of relatives and friends.

As he sat down, he watched Mannering impassively; then beckoned. Cyrus dropped behind, as if to make sure Mannering was now very much on his own.

Mannering stopped a few feet in front of the desk.

"Good afternoon, Mr. Ballas," he said.

"So you are John Mannering," said Mario Ballas. His

voice was soft, with a noticeable, quite attractive accent; there was even the hint of a lisp. "I have often wanted to meet you, but there is so little time. So very little time." He made the words sound like a sighing : "So ver' leet'el time". He smiled, as if with great effort; then raised his hands, which had the same wax-like appearance as his face, in a gesture which encompassed the whole room and all that was in it. "Now we have met it is on a very serious matter. I wish you to understand, Mr. Mannering, that if it were necessary, I would give up every single thing in this room— *every one*, Mr. Mannering—for the microfilm which Professor Alundo owned and which you now possess. It is so exceedingly valuable to me." He paused, then added with curiously steel-like emphasis: "You understand, no doubt, how determined I am to obtain that microfilm. *No one* is going to prevent me from getting it. No one—and nothing."

CHAPTER TWELVE

Bad Man With a Cause

MARIO BALLAS stopped speaking, but did not look away.

Mannering felt the impact of the words, the threat implied, the ultimatum. Nothing and no one was going to prevent this man from getting that film. *Why?* Why could it be so precious to him? Why was he so sure of its value? And how was Professor Alundo involved in this strange battle for possession?

"Do you understand me?" Ballas demanded softly. "I would give up every one of the rare and priceless things in this room for the microfilm. *Do* you understand?"

"Yes," Mannering said; yet he did not truly understand.

"Where is the microfilm, Mannering?"

Mannering countered, after a pause : "Why do you want it, Senor Ballas?" The 'Senor' came quite naturally. He heard a rustle of movement behind him but paid no attention.

"That is my business," Mario Ballas said.

"If I knew why you wanted it I might help you to find it," Mannering answered quietly.

"You know where it is. You will help me to get it."

Mannering smiled faintly.

"You think I do, Senor. But must we waste time? I assure you in all earnestness that I won't lift a finger to help you find the microfilm, until I know what is in it."

He heard Cyrus catch his breath, and saw Ballas glance towards the man as if forbidding any kind of interruption.

The wax-like hands were placed palm downwards on the table; the lean body did not change position.

"And if you know this, you will help me?"

"If I like your reason for wanting it, yes," Mannering told him.

"Mr. Mannering," said Mario Ballas, "no one knows that you are here in Mexico. No one will ever see you leave, whether you are alive or dead. It would be very easy to kill you, and the dying could be very, very painful."

Mannering said: "I see." He shifted his position, and heard another rustle behind him. The older man watched. There was no other sound in the room, no distraction. "Senor Ballas," Mannering went on, "you have a reputation for being a cold-blooded killer. You are hated and you are feared. But *I* don't hate you—and I don't fear you. And there is no way you can make me do anything I do not wish to do."

After a long, tense pause, Ballas stirred.

"You know so much," he said.

"I know enough."

"You would talk, as everyone else has talked."

"It wouldn't help you," Mannering said.

"Explain that, please."

"I cannot tell you where to find the microfilm. I can only help you to find it. If you kill me, you will lose every chance you have, because"—very softly and deliberately Mannering made his final throw—"*only* I can help. *Only* I know the clues."

"You speak as if this were a game."

"I carry out all my investigations as if they were games. It is far more absorbing that way."

"So very English," Ballas said. "English enough to be the truth. And I have heard that the famous John Mannering never takes anything seriously." He appeared to brood, and Mannering believed he was making up his mind whether to try to make him talk—by torture, beyond any doubt—or whether to take his word. So much of what he had said was true that all of it might be convincing. If this old man, so used to having his own way and to having men cringe before him, could listen to reason, Mannering believed that he might win.

It was almost as if no one else was in the room.

"Mr. Mannering," Ballas said, "you are an English gentleman." He paused. "You were *born* an English gentleman." The second pause was longer and Mannering could not guess what was to follow; could it be the axiom that an Englishman's word was his bond? Or that they should reach a gentleman's agreement? "In politics, you are an Independent—you see how closely I have checked on your history. Are these things true?"

"Yes."

"What do *you* mean by 'Independent'?"

"Freedom from any political party," Mannering said, trying to understand the reasons for this new subject. "There's so much bad and too little good in party thinking—and that goes for all parties."

"For them *all*?" echoed Ballas. "*All?*"

That was a remarkable moment. For the first time his voice rose as if in incredulity, and his eyes glinted. There were spots of glowing red on his cheeks. Mannering had seen such manifestations before—had seen them in fanatical politicians who went almost mad when they were discussing politics, who lost their self-control the moment their opinions were contradicted. He had a prickly feeling at the back of his neck, knowing that something very startling was simmering in the mind of this strange man.

"For them *all*?" repeated Ballas. "You *mean* that?"

"In some you have to look a long way to find the good," Mannering conceded.

"Ah ha!" exclaimed Ballas, in the tones of one who has

spent much time and trouble in endeavouring to trip up his opponent and has at last succeeded. "Are you telling me that you, an English gentleman, born in the tradition of British freedom, a man from the land of the Mother of Parliaments, a man in whose land the Magna Carta was signed, believe there is *any* good—however little—in—*Communism*?"

In that last word there was deadly venom which came out as if ejected by a snake. Mannering was astounded, and very watchful. He was fully aware that he was still groping for the truth, that if he said the wrong thing, the result could be disastrous.

Ballas sat, his arrogant indifference fallen from him, his fingers interlaced and strained white at the knuckles. Mannering tried not to show the tension he himself was feeling, by standing in an easy and relaxed position; in point of fact, he had never wanted to sit down more.

"Answer me," Ballas said at last. "Do you see *any* good in Communism?"

"In its intent," Mannering said, cautiously.

"You are a fool. There is only evil in it !"

Mannering said : "It was born out of evil conditions, Senor."

"Are you defending it?" hissed Ballas.

"I'm condemning the conditions which gave it birth," Mannering said. He was sweating.

"It is evil, I tell you. Evil, corrupt, horrible ! It will suffocate mankind."

Ballas sat back in his golden chair, surrounded by the riches and beauty won by his crimes, his ruthlessness—and his lips trembled and his voice quivered; even his hands shook on the desk, his jewelled cufflinks tapping a menacing tattoo.

Mannering said: "But at least it tried to let all men breathe."

"You are playing with words!"

"I always play, remember," Mannering said. "I never take anything seriously. You told me so."

"Mannering! Are you a Communist?"

"I certainly am not."

"Then why are you helping Communists in their foul work?" Ballas raised his hands from the desk and slapped them down on it, furiously. "Answer me! If you are not one, why do you help them? Answer me, or you will wish you had never been born!"

The lost youth of the man, the uncouthness of his early upbringing, the latent savagery in him, all showed in what he said and the way he said it; the veneer of culture melted away and the ugliness beneath was left exposed. In an instant he might give the order which would throw Mannering to the vicious cruelties of his trained thugs.

Mannering, though fearfully conscious that danger hung over him by a thread, became increasingly aware that something else lay beneath this anger.

There was some other, finer quality in this man—and Mannering felt kinship with that quality. He understood and shared his passion for the *objets d'art* about them, that knowledge of their need for care, in fact, for love. There were two, at least two, aspects in Mario Ballas; ugliness and beauty went side by side, in places overlapping. Mannering could not hope to influence the evil in the man except through that which was good.

"Mannering," Ballas said with ominous calm, "I am waiting for your answer."

"I wonder," Mannering said, 'whether you have ever been to Russia—to Moscow."

Hatred sparkled in Ballas's eyes, but he did not speak.

"In the palaces of the Kremlin, the cathedrals and the Armoury, they have treasures which would not be out of place in this room. They venerate them, too. When are you going to learn that nothing is all bad?"

"It is a foul régime!"

"So was Britain's, a thousand years ago."

Voice quivering, hands now clenched, Ballas spat: "You *are* a Communist."

Very levelly, Mannering said: "I am no more a Communist than you are an honest man."

Again Cyrus caught his breath; fear and tension were in the room.

Mannering moved for the first time, sideways and slightly backwards, to a carved wooden chair with tapestry back and deep red velvet seat. He lowered himself, fingers resting lightly on the delicately chiselled figures of snakes and animals which formed the two arm-rests. He moved with great deliberation and did not once take his gaze off Maria Ballas. As his body slackened, he realised how tense he had been, and how afraid he was, even now. But nothing of this showed. He did not know how long he sat watching, sensing that Ballas was fighting some strange battle within himself.

The man named Cyrus looked on, as if mesmerised.

Cyrus Lake was unbelieving.

This Englishman had talked to Mario Ballas as no one living had ever talked to him. For less, for half as much frankness, he had waved his hand and by so doing condemned men to their ruin; to their death. For a quarter of a century he had assumed the position of absolute ruler within his own sphere. He had built a wall about himself which had virtually put him beyond the law, and had amassed a fabulous fortune; because of this he had been fawned upon and almost worshipped. Cyrus Lake knew that there was a hideous quality in him, yet also a magnetic one which attracted men so that they not only served him loyally but believed in him.

Now, expecting an outburst of terrible wrath, Cyrus watched the conflict that was taking place; and he sensed an unbelievable thing—that for once in his life Mario Ballas was torn by doubt. Watching the struggle between good and evil, he knew only that for Mario it was like a struggle between life and death.

Whereas Mannering —

The remarkable Englishman who had quelled Tiger O'Leary with a contemptuous word, was leaning comfortably back in a chair in which no one but Mario ever sat, looking calm and unperturbed.

Slowly, awfully, the silent storm died down.

Slowly, Ballas raised his right hand. Daring to move at last, Cyrus went swiftly to an Elizabethan corner cupboard, taking out a decanter of whisky and silver bowl of ice. He brought two glasses to the desk, poured whisky over three glistening ice cubes and gave the glass to his master. Mario took it and waved again, this time to Mannering.

Cyrus said huskily: "On the rocks, Mr. Mannering?"

"No, thanks. Straight."

Whisky gurgled. Cyrus gave Mannering his drink, but did not pour one for himself. Ballas was already drinking. Mannering, sipping, dared to hope, even to believe, that the crisis was past. The old man drank slowly, the spots of red still glowing brightly in his cheeks. When he spoke again his voice was mellowed; in a way he looked older.

"How much do you know about me, Mannering?"

"As much as the British police and the American newspapers know."

Ballas smiled faintly, perhaps contemptuously, perhaps with pride.

"Don't you think they know everything about me?"

"No."

"Why not?"

"They don't have a good word to say for you," Mannering answered.

Ballas stared expressionlessly for a long time—then broke into a dry laugh.

Mannering glanced at Cyrus Lake, whose eyes were cast down, as if such a revelation was improper for him to witness.

"So they don't have a good word for me—but *you* do. Is that it?"

"I have a good word for anyone who can surround himself with these things, no matter how he got them."

"I *bought* them."

"I know—I supplied some of them." Mannering pointed to a Genoese figurine. "That, for instance. And the Ming vase. And the Egyptian goblet." He mentioned ten of the pieces before him, including an Aztec jewelled axe. "I didn't realise they were for you, you use several buying agents, don't you?"

"Certainly."

"So that you don't let the world know how wealthy you are?"

"They can guess," Ballas said, with a shrug. "They cannot know. *You* know. Probably more than anyone living, you know the value of these possessions of mine. Do you remember what I said just now?"

"That you would exchange them all for the microfilm."

"Yes," Ballas said. "And that is the truth."

"How can the microfilm be worth so much?"

"That is a good question," Ballas said, and went on slowly, as if intent on making every word meaningful and true. "Mr. Mannering, you are an Englishman and I am an American. You do not have to approve of the way I have made my money or the way I live. You do not have to believe, as I do, that some men are kings and some are cattle, and that the lives of the cattle are unimportant. But you will be a fool if you believe that the Russian or the Chinese way of life is as good as ours. I *believe* in America, Mr. Mannering. Just as Hitler believed in Germany and Caesar believed in Rome, I believe in America. I will give all I have to preserve it. I hope you believe me; I hope you believe that."

Mannering drew a long, slow breath, surprised and yet not surprised; and, in a strange way, deeply touched.

"I believe you," he said simply.

"Then also believe that the microfilm you are preserving for the man Alundo could destroy America, and all our Western way of life. Now *there* is your evil man, Mr. Mannering. *There* is your evil incarnate. Professor Arthur Alundo. I believe he is the most evil man alive."

CHAPTER THIRTEEN

Break-Out

BALLAS'S words seemed to echo and re-echo in Mannering's mind. "Now there is your evil man, Mr. Mannering. *There* is your evil incarnate. Professor Arthur Alundo. I believe he is the most evil man alive." There could be no doubt that Ballas meant exactly what he said.

Gradually a mental picture came to Mannering—not of Alundo but of his daughter, Ethel. If she were here, what would she do? Or say?

Did the accusation make any sense at all?

Ballas raised his hand again, and Cyrus refilled his glass. "You heard me, Mr. Mannering?"

"Yes, I heard you. But I've also been told that Alundo is a man of peace."

"He is a man who will sell his country, even the whole of the West. That makes him a traitor. Do you know what I would do with traitors?"

Mannering said dryly: "What you would do with cattle, presumably. I doubt if Alundo would willingly kill a fly. And you—how many men have you killed, or had killed? Ten? Twenty? A hundred? If you were both on trial, he for treason and you for murder, he would be exonerated and you would be found guilty. I doubt if you could even buy yourself a reprieve."

He was taking a chance, a desperate chance, of angering the old man and risking an outburst of rage. But the calm of Ballas remained unbroken.

"Justice is blind," he said.

"And the law is an ass, I know that one too. What makes you think Alundo is a traitor?"

"Don't pretend you don't know."

"Senor Ballas," Mannering said coldly, "I don't expect you to lie to me and I won't lie to you. I know nothing, apart from what I have read in the newspapers, about Alundo—I know nothing about the microfilm. I came to America to find the Fentham necklace and bracelet—which I have strong reason to believe were stolen by your nephew Enrico—and also to bring a small collection of Mexican *objets d'art* to the HemisFair in San Antonio. Your nephew led me to Alundo and his daughter. Until she told me about a mysterious package, I knew nothing about it. Why is this film so important? What *is* it all about?"

Ballas was drinking his second whisky more slowly.

"You did not come to Chicago to seek me out?"

"I came to try to discover the missing pieces of jewellery, which I understood had been stolen by your nephew. I assumed they were for your collection." Mannering glanced towards the nearer showcase, filled with diamonds, emeralds, rubies and sapphires.

Ballas said very slowly:

"For my collection—yes, I suppose so. Yes." He paused. "I am coming to trust you, Mr. Mannering, to believe you are a truthful man. You really do not know why the micro-film is so important, do you?"

"No," Mannering said. "Why is it, Senor?"

With great deliberation, Mario Ballas answered: "It is the record of a scientific discovery—a discovery which could be used as a weapon to destroy America—to destroy the whole world."

Mannering absorbed this statement slowly, pondering with one part of his mind, as he asked:

"Who made this discovery — and what, actually, has been discovered?"

"A scientist in an Anglo-American research company discovered it by accident, as so many vital discoveries are made. It is the introduction of a gas into the air which destroys the oxygen. So, people suffocate. Once released in any area, the effect is cumulative and expanding—it cannot be stopped."

As Ballas talked, the light in the room dimmed as if a great shadow had covered the sky; the shutters were in fact sliding silently over the windows with almost theatrical precision. Cyrus moved, and Mannering saw him put a box on a small stand.

". . . the scientist who discovered this, made a precise record of all the experiments which led up to the discovery, and reported to a colleague. The two men repeated the experiments several times in sealed rooms, always with the same result. Convinced that this secret must be kept, they agreed to destroy all records of the weapon. One believed they were destroyed, but the other took a film of the records. I want you to see part of it for yourself, Mr. Mannering."

A movie-projector suddenly shone its bright beam on to a screen. A coloured picture appeared—of mice, then of cats, then of rats; whole colonies of them. One moment they were alive, moving, busy, eager to find food; the next they were gasping, tumbling about, writhing—and suddenly they were still.

Mannering felt touched by the horror of what he saw.

"Mr. Mannering," Ballas began again in a measured voice, "that can happen to all mankind if this secret is ever released—which it can be, by Professor Alundo." The old man's gaze was unwavering. "The research worker concerned was an associate of Alundo's in a Peace Movement. He made a copy of the film and gave both copy and original to Alundo. *Listen*."

There was a click.

Then, a voice sounded—obviously on tape. A man spoke, gasping, as if afraid; tormented.

"I gave them to Alundo—yes, *both* copies . . . No, there are no others . . . Yes, the gas can be made very simply if you know the basic secret . . . A little released in any area will kill everyone in it, and will spread until it can be sealed off—and only the oceans and deserts can seal it off. If you had seen those mice and rats . . . No, there *are* only two copies. I don't *know* what Alundo did with them . . . *I tell you I gave them to Professor Alundo.* I— No . . . No. . . !"

The man screamed.

The tape recorder stopped abruptly.

Mario Ballas said : "Such a man had to die, Mr. Mannering. The other research worker also died. I had been watching Alundo very closely, and after they had met, I had this man questioned—as you heard. What he said was true—he did give both copies of the microfilm to Alundo. Alundo gave one of these copies to a friend for safe keeping—that copy I have already secured. But Alundo still has the other. We do not understand the formula shown on the film—only research physicists can do so. Our American physicists, or Russia's. Or China's. I do not believe that *anyone* should ever be able to possess such a weapon. The secret must be destroyed." After a long, tense pause, Ballas went on softly: "Don't you agree, Mannering?"

"If it is all you say it is—yes, I do," Mannering said slowly.

"It *is* all I say. And so long as Alundo has his copy of the film, God knows what might not happen!" Ballas's voice sharpened, touched again with anger. "He preaches peace and deals in war. You talk to me about the few people I have killed. My God, a man like Alundo will see millions dead, in the name of peace!" For the first time, Ballas began to push his chair back, and immediately Cyrus moved to help him; so Cyrus was a personal servant as well as a personal bodyguard.

Ballas hardly seemed aware that his man was there, He moved slowly, and Mannering realised that he was very, very old.

"I know exactly what I am doing," Ballas asserted. "In the past, I have acted blindly. I killed men because they were in my way. But not these days—never, these days. If I order a man to be killed it is for a purpose I believe in." He stood in front of Mannering, speaking with quiet vehemence: "I kill no man without giving him warning and an opportunity to change. You think of me as a murderer, but a hundred dependents of men I have killed come to me for their livelihood. Ask Cyrus Lake—Cyrus! How many years have you worked for me?"

"Twenty-seven," Cyrus answered.

"And do I ill-treat you? Do you live in fear of me? I command you—tell Mannering the truth."

"I don't fear you," Cyrus said. "I serve you."

"And there are hundreds like him, their wives and families dependent on me, confident I will treat them well and fairly. Have I ever given you a raw deal, Cyrus?"

"Never, Mario."

"Or anyone who served me loyally?"

"Each according to his deserts," Cyrus said; and Mannering accepted the statement with the simplicity with which it had been uttered.

"Judge for yourself." Ballas was walking about now, very slowly and awkwardly, carried away by what he was saying. "I am not a cruel man although sometimes I have to be cruel. I am not a hard man although sometimes I have to be hard. Do you know *this*, Mannering. Apart from the great foundations, like Ford and Rockefeller, I give more money to good causes than anyone else in America. Cancer research, heart diseases, the poor, the sick—I am a great giver,

Mannering. Do you think any of those I have robbed would give so generously?"

It was obvious that an answer was expected.

"I doubt it," Mannering said.

"You are right to doubt it. Each —" Ballas broke off, looking straight at Mannering. "I tell you Alundo is a hypocrite and a fraud, and a deadly danger to the American way of life for so long as he has that microfilm. I must have Alundo's copy, Mannering, and I mean to obtain it. There are only these two copies in existence. One I have—and to obtain possession of the other I will, if necessary, kill, torture, maim, spend all my fortune. Only when both copies are destroyed will there be no danger to America—or to Britain—or to the world. Where is it, Mannering? I have been patient with you, because there is some quality in you which I like, but—where is it, Mannering? To find it, I will tear your body apart."

Mannering had no doubt at all that he would.

"I will help you find it," he said, stiffly. "When —"

"There must be no conditions!"

"But there are conditions," Mannering said.

"Are you deaf? Didn't you hear what I said I would do to you?"

"You can't get Alundo's copy without me," Mannering retorted; but his heart was thumping. "If you keep me a prisoner here, you will have no hope at all of getting it. I've told you that. I will help you find it as soon as I believe you're right about Professor Alundo. I want to talk to him."

Ballas gasped: "Are you mad?"

"Are you going to let me leave here?"

"Not until I have the film!"

Mannering eyed the old man levelly for a few moments, then turned to Cyrus.

"May I have another whisky?"

"Sure."

"I mean what I say," Ballas insisted. "It is quite impossible for you to get out of this house alive without my permission. And if you do get out, a barren land stretches for a hundred miles in all directions. You would perish."

"Whisky helps me to think," Mannering said. He waited until Cyrus came with the glass, took it—and before the man could move away, seized his wrist in an agonising grip. At the same time, he jumped up, and flung the whisky straight into Ballas's face. As the old man staggered back, Mannering spun Cyrus round, then chopped the edge of his free hand down on the nape of the man's neck. Cyrus did not even groan as he dropped to the floor. Mannering sprang at Ballas, who was groping blindly for the other side of the desk where, possibly, there was a hidden alarm. It wasn't pleasant to ill-treat an old man, but Mannering dealt as summarily with him as he had dealt with Cyrus.

Ballas dropped like a stone; suddenly, the room was silent.

Mannering straightened Cyrus's body and ran through his pockets, finding nothing of interest until he came to a small leather case, rather like a key-case. Inside was a tiny, fine-pointed awl, and a small phial, sealed with plastic, containing a colourless liquid. Mannering had no doubt these were the knockout drops. He unstopped the phial, dipped the point of the awl inside, and then pressed it on to the inside of Cyrus's forearm. The arm fell limp. Then he did the same to Ballas. Standing up, he carefully replaced both stopper and awl, closed the leather case and slipped it into his breast pocket.

Now, virtually alone, he was still in acute danger.

He might even be watched at this moment.

He did not think it likely—surely, if anyone *had* been watching, an alarm would have been raised?—but there was no certainty. He looked about the room and up into the raftered ceiling, examining its supporting beams.

There *could* be spy-holes in any of these; and others, round the walls.

He moved towards the door through which he had come. Was it self-opening? Or was there some trick? It could be electronically controlled; it was even possible it was protected by a ray. There was such treasure in this room—treasure measured in tens of millions of pounds. No risks would be taken with it.

Mannering studied the door. It appeared, from inside the room, to be made of brass-studded wood, but Mannering felt sure it was of metal, almost certainly bullet- and sound-proof, and possibly impervious to fire. Neither of the men had touched it—ah! It had been closed from the outside. And locked? If *he* owned such treasures as these, and had two guards outside, what would he do?

With half of his mind he was calculating how long he had before these two men came round. Not much more than half-an-hour, he judged. That should be time enough. He studied the big, brass lock, and the three bolts, one at the top, one at the bottom, one in the middle. All were shot, so they must close automatically to lock people both in and out. There must be a control both inside and outside the room.

What would *he* do? He would have a buzzer at the desk, one which could be manually operated. *One buzz: come in. Two: I'm coming out.* And now he recalled the buzz when the lock was released and he and Cyrus had been admitted. That had been *one* buzz. His heart began to beat very fast. He reached the far side of the desk, and lowered himself into the golden chair. There was no bell push in sight. He ran his fingers gingerly along the desk's underledge, but found nothing. He examined the floor, and then shook his head. It wouldn't be there. Ballas's legs were too short.

The chair itself?

It would have to be somewhere within easy reach of right

or left hand. How had the man drunk his whisky? Right-handed? A right-handed man often had the bell pushes, telephone and gadgets on his left, so that he could write and talk freely at the same time.

The telephones *were* on the left.

Mannering began to run his fingers along the jewelled arms, remembering that the spot, when he found it—*if* he found it—would be within easy reach of the small, slightly built man who ruled his empire from this chair. And it would not be a spot which one could touch easily by accident: it would be under the seat, perhaps?—or at the side? Mannering ran his fingers along the golden underledges, and found several round protuberances; in a lesser chair these would be the small, undecorated heads of nails, or tacks; here, each was a study, smooth, polished, beautifully engraved. He stood up, tilted the chair to one side, and saw that there were five, all gold, all delicately chased. The most convenient to touch would be the middle one. But before he pressed it, he had to be ready to act.

If he were right, there would be a buzz of sound and the door would open. He wanted to be able to press and be at the door almost at one and the same moment. Looking down at the floor, Mannering saw that the chair was wired to the wall, and that there was little slack. So he couldn't move the chair nearer to the door. Turning to the desk, he managed to shift this a few inches so that now there was nothing between the door and himself, then stood as far away from the chair as he could, while still being able to press the middle stud. Arm stretched out, finger at the third protuberance, he pressed.

The buzzer sounded at the door.

Mannering flung himself across the room, one hand at the pocket where he had put the leather case containing the awl. As he reached the door, it began to open.

A man appeared, his face set in expectancy; it was the

kind of expression one might assume for Ballas. It changed ludicrously at sight of Mannering, and the man's right hand darted towards his left shoulder; his gun.

Mannering kicked him in the pit of the stomach.

The man gasped, and staggered back. As he did so, Mannering thrust him to one side, and leapt to the landing.

On the right, halfway towards the door, stood Tiger O'Leary.

Mannering saw the glint in O'Leary's eyes, that unmistakable look of evil, saw it change on the instant to one of gloating, almost of satisfaction. He also saw the gun halfway from O'Leary's shoulder holster, and knew that he had no time to reach the man before he fired.

His fingers closed round the awl. Snatching it from his pocket, he flung it towards O'Leary.

He saw the man flinch, but he did not back away; it was unlikely that he realised what was coming.

The awl struck his cheek.

O'Leary winced at the sharp pain and lost a split second's advantage as Mannering closed with him in a desperate attempt to prevent him from shooting. One shot, however wide, would be enough to raise the alarm. Mannering gripped the other's gun wrist, and twisted—but even as he did so, O'Leary went limp and began to sag at the knees. Slowly he slithered to the floor, leaving the gun in Mannering's hand.

Mannering put it in his pocket, bent down, and dragged O'Leary's body into the big room. The man he had kicked, inert but not wholly unconscious, offered no immediate threat; nevertheless it would not be long before he was sufficiently recovered to shout for help. Mannering recovered the awl, re-dipped it into the phial, and pressed it firmly into his arm. Now, he was on his own.

The door was still open.

He went out on to the landing, walked swiftly to the head of the stairs, and looked down. The Reynolds and two Rubens seemed to look down with him.

Nothing stirred.

Cautiously he descended the stairs, the thick carpet muffling all sound. No one appeared. Walking quickly through the hallway, he came, once again, to the front door.

He turned the handle—and there in front of him was the courtyard.

He walked out, pulling the door to behind him. He remembered exactly the position of the three aircraft, as he hurried towards an open archway. He saw no one. The sun struck very hot on the back of his head. He reached an outer courtyard, where several dogs lay in the shade, and a very old man with a face as dark and lined as carved wood sat dozing. Ignoring him, Mannering went through a second archway.

The three aeroplanes stood unattended, not far from two concrete landing strips.

Mannering turned towards them. The first he came to was a Chipmunk, and he had flown the model often enough to be sure he could fly this one—if it were ready for flight. He stepped into the welcome shade of the aeroport, and pulled the chocks from the wheels.

As he did so, he heard the sound of an approaching aircraft.

Swinging himself quickly into the cockpit, he pulled the starter ring, praying the engine would start at once; and it did. He took two precious minutes to make sure there was plenty of fuel and to refresh his mind about the controls. Then, looking into the sky, he saw a twin-engined aircraft coming in. He began to taxi. Behind him, two men wearing sombreros but dressed in mechanics' overalls, emerged from the outbuildings. One of them began to run after Mannering; and to shout and gesticulate.

Mannering actually laughed.

As his machine gathered speed, slowly, gloriously rising from the ground as if he had been used to handling her all his life, he felt a wild surge of exhilaration. He had achieved the impossible—he *had* escaped.

Soon, he was at eight hundred feet, and circling. He needed to head north for the United States, and he wondered how far it was away. Seeing a pair of fieldglasses hanging from the instrument panel, he focused them on the arriving aircraft, which had just landed. A man jumped out of it, staring up at Mannering.

It was Alundo's friend—'Texas Tommy' Ricardi.

CHAPTER FOURTEEN

HemisFair

EVERYWHERE Mannering looked, there was the barren, scrub-speckled rock on which nothing seemed to move. The sun was almost directly behind him as he headed due north. He had no idea of the distance to the border, but a chart stuck to the door showed that a place marked with a cross, on the Mexican side, was about fifty miles from a small river town; that would be the Rio Grande. Mannering was troubled only by one thing : that he might be followed, might even be shot down.

He was not followed.

He flew over the narrow river which did not look wide enough to be the Rio Grande, but it was. Glancing at the chart, he saw a second cross, at a place called Del Rio, and a third, much larger; this was San Antonio.

"At least the HemisFair people know of me," he said aloud. "It's only a hundred or so miles away."

Now that the excitement and tension were over, he felt curiously limp, his mind drained of all emotion; but he remembered very clearly all that Ballas had said about Professor Alundo.

A laconic voice sounded over the radio.

"You want to come in? . . . You sure can . . . Strip seventeen . . . You see it? . . . Okay, glad to have you with us. If we need you again we'll call you Flight 0075."

Mannering found himself smiling, because the voice sounded so casual. He kept the radio on, in case of any change of instructions, and looked about him. The city sprawled in all directions, the land surrounding it varying from green to yellow; this was very different from the barren rocky land he had left. He saw the criss-cross of streets and the moving traffic, then turned to come in for landing and saw what appeared to be a huge map like the one marked HEMISFAIR NINETY-TWO ACRES on the wall of Ricardi's room.

What was Ricardi doing at Ballas's house?

Mannering pushed that thought out of his mind and studied the Exhibition Grounds. The buildings were sharply defined, clean and new. A great tower overlorded them all, close by a huge arena. Dotted about everywhere, he could see men working at tremendous speed : they were only six days off the official opening by the President of the United States.

Was it simply coincidence that Alundo was to speak here?

What would happen if that formula on the microfilm were known—and used, say, in the great auditorium where he was to give his lecture?

Deeply troubled, Mannering thrust this thought away.

It was time for landing.

A small van drove towards and kept pace with him as he brought the plane to a standstill. When he got out, a mechanic was there to meet him with a casual "Howdy?" He pointed towards the offices. A huge sign saying HEMIS-FAIR OFFICIALS was on one side. As Mannering went towards this, he was intercepted by a pleasant looking girl.

"Did you tell Flight Control you were from Mexico, sir?"

"Yes. But I've nothing to declare."

"If you will just attend to the formalities, sir . . ."

There was a cursory examination and a welcome: "Glad to have you in San Antonio, Mr. Mannering," and then the

E

girl escorted him to the HemisFair offices. Everything was pleasant, orderly, under control.

"We have so many visitors by air we have a special section for them here at the airport, sir . . . Mr. Who? . . . Mr. Mannering? *Mannering?* You mean from London, England . . . We have an exhibit from you !" The clerk's eyes lit up with interest, quite suddenly Mannering was treated as a celebrity. "If there is anything we can do, sir . . . Yes, sir, Mr. Steven Marshall is in Austin right now but he'll be glad to see you when he gets back . . . Yes, sir, your exhibits arrived safely . . . Yes, sir, there are flights from here to Chicago non-stop . . . Yes, sir, you surely can use a room with a telephone . . ."

First, Mannering washed, had a light meal at a coffee shop, then went to a small room set aside for visitors who had come on HemisFair business. He was new enough to the practice of dialling long distance numbers to be startled when the Palmer House Hotel in Chicago came on the line almost as soon as he finished dialling.

". . . we *may* have a room, sir, we have the Mid-West Cotton Packers Convention here and are fully booked, but . . . If you will wait a moment, sir."

Mannering waited two minutes before they promised him a room on the third floor.

He rang off, and called Registration at the Conrad Hilton.

"Why, surely, Mr. Mannering, there are some messages for you . . . Would you care to have me read them . . . I certainly will, sir . . . Miss Ethel Alundo tried to reach you twice, and will call later . . . Mr. Ricardi called last night, no message . . . Mrs. Mannering of Green Street, London, England, called, will you telephone as soon as you can, it doesn't matter what time . . ." The girl's tone changed. "They're later than we are, sir, because of the time zones . . . And will you call Mr. Mario Ballas, sir, at La Racienda, Mexicali 7–3142."

"What time did that call come in?" Mannering asked
sharply.

"It's marked two-fifty-five, only a few minutes ago. That's
all the messages, sir."

"Thank you very much," Mannering said. He rang off,
glancing at his watch and confirming that it was nearly three
o'clock; that meant it would be eight o'clock in England. He
put in a call for Lorna, then leaned back in his chair, wondering first what his wife, and then what Ballas wanted.
What *could* the old man want? Not to plead, but possibly to
reason—more likely to threaten. How could he threaten
now? Mannering leaned across and put in a call to Ricardi's
flat. It rang for a long time, but there was no answer—so
Professor Alundo wasn't in, either, mused Mannering. He
could picture Ricardi at Ballas's Mexico home. Was he a
regular visitor? Were they in league with each other?

But it was too easy, too often fatal, to jump to conclusions.
Why had *Ethel* called him?

He lifted the receiver, dialled O, then asked for Mexicali
7–3142. He had a curious sense of apprehension as he waited
for the ringing sound. He did not have to wait long before
a man answered; and at the sound of the voice, Mannering
realised that during the whole of his stay at La Racienda,
he had not once heard, or seen, a woman.

The man said : "Who is that?"

"John Mannering," said Mannering.

There was a strange inflection in the other's voice.

"Mannering? It's a good thing you called !"

"Mr. Ballas called me," Mannering said coldly.

"Just hold on," the speaker said; there was no doubt of
his rising excitement.

Suddenly there was a scuffling sound at the other end of
the wire, and a dull thud; Mannering thought he heard a
sharp cry of pain. Then a woman's voice rang clearly over
the line. "Don't hit him, please don't hit him. Don't —"

There was a shout, a slap, and more confused sounds, as Mannering's fingers tightened on the receiver. At last he had heard a woman's voice at the Mexican house; and he knew that Ethel Alundo was there, apparently in great trouble.

Was he supposed to hold on? Would anyone else speak? These and a dozen other questions flashed through Mannering's mind as he waited. There were no sounds in the room, none from outside, and those at the other end of the line faded into silence, although he did not hear the telephone being replaced.

Then, very softly, Mario Ballas's voice spoke.

"You are a fool, Mr. Mannering."

"Who am I to argue?" Mannering answered. "If Ethel Alundo isn't here in two hours' time, I shall send for the police and report exactly what has happened."

"And if you send for the police, they will be told that Ethel Alundo, a guest in my house, was caught red-handed trying to break into my gallery. The police won't help her, Mr. Mannering, or help you."

That was probably true.

"Mr. Mannering," Ballas went on, "I intend to get that microfilm. Bring it to me, and the girl will not be hurt. I want it by this time tomorrow. Fly to any airport in Texas and telephone me. I will send for you. If you do as I tell you, neither you nor Alundo's daughter have anything to fear. If you don't, the girl —"

He deliberately left the sentence hanging in the air, like a threat.

Mannering said thinly : "Don't hurt her."

"That is entirely up to you."

"Don't hurt her, or you will never get the film."

"Mannering," Ballas said evenly, "I am too mature a man to be influenced by sentimentality. This young woman means nothing to me. A hundred like her are maimed or killed on the roads every day, a hundred like her are being introduced to drugs, a hundred like her will be raped before the day is out. She is a pawn in this grave affair, unimportant and insignificant. She may be important to her father or her lover—even to you : but she is not important to me."

"Lover?" Mannering echoed.

"Lover," repeated Ballas. "His name is Ricardi. Remember, I want the film by tomorrow night."

He rang off.

Mannering replaced the receiver very slowly, staring at the wall. He could picture Ballas, Ethel, Ricardi and Alundo, yet none of them seemed sharp in his mind's eye—except Ballas. The cold-blooded way the old man talked made one thing crystal clear : the issues were too great for him even to consider the human factors.

Now, he had Ethel prisoner.

Was Ricardi her lover? Mannering had believed her when she had said she had never been to New York before, but she could have been lying; she and her father might both be deeply involved. What had Ballas called Alundo? "Now there is your evil man, Mr. Mannering, *there* is your evil incarnate."

Was it possible —?

Mannering forced himself not to dwell on it, but dialled Chicago Whitehall 4–31495 again. He hardly expected an answer, but the ringing sound stopped almost at once and Alundo said brusquely :

"Hallo? Who is that?"

"This is Mannering —" Mannering began.

"Mannering!" cried Alundo. "I have been trying to get you all day, where—oh, it doesn't matter, the only thing that matters is Ethel. She's been kidnapped!" His voice rose. "D'you hear me? Ethel has been kidnapped! You've got to find her. Understand? You've got to find her. Don't lose a minute, Mannering."

Mannering said quietly : "Where is she?"

"I don't know."

"Have you told the police?"

"Police? Don't be a maniac, of course I haven't ! This isn't a matter for the police, far too much is at stake. Find her, Mannering."

An operator's voice broke in:

"Excuse me, Mr. Mannering, but your call to London is through."

"I'll take it," Mannering said. "Alundo, wait in the apartment until I contact you again. Get off the line now." Alundo began to say something, but was cut off, and almost immediately Mannering heard Lorna's voice.

"John ! Are you there—*John!*"

"Hallo, darling," Mannering said. "It's good to hear you."

"Good," breathed Lorna. "Darling, what have you been up to? Bristow's been to see me. He's had a request from the Chicago Police Department for a full dossier on you in connection with the murder of a man named Enrico Ballas. He thinks they're going to arrest you—he really thinks so. John, what *is* happening? *Do* you know anything about the murder of this man?"

"Enough to be charged with it," Mannering said dryly. "No need for you to worry, though, I —"

"No need to worry ! I'm off my head with anxiety. Bristow said that this man Ballas is the son or nephew or something of one of the most dangerous men in America."

"And so he was," Mannering said. "But there's still no need for you to worry." He racked his brains for something to tell her that might keep her from fretting. An idea came almost on the instant; he pounced on it with alacrity. "There's one thing you can do to help."

"Anything!" Hope rose in Lorna's voice of settled despondency.

"Dr. Arthur Alundo has a daughter, Ethel —"

"What has Alundo to do with this?"

"You'd be surprised! Find out where Ethel lives, what she does for a living, whether she's engaged or has a boy-friend, particularly an American boy-friend. Get Josh to help." Josh Larraby was the manager of his Mayfair shop; it had been he who had told Mannering of the rumour that Enrico Ballas had stolen Fentham's jewels.

"Yes. Yes, I will. But —"

"Find out everything you possibly can about the girl," Mannering went on, "and telephone me at the Palmer House —"

"Where?"

"The Palmer—P-A-L-M-E-R–House Hotel, Chicago. If I'm not there, try the Conrad Hilton. But darling, how are *you*?"

"Not terribly keen on being a widow! They still have the death penalty over there."

"It depends on what State Ballas was murdered in, but don't worry about the death penalty, just find out all you can about Ethel Alundo."

"I will. Oh, there's another thing! Bristow said that Donald Hennessy is in Chicago—he thought you'd like to know."

"That might be very useful," Mannering said appreciatively.

Hennessy was a Home Office official who often worked with Scotland Yard, and was an old friend of Mannering.

"John," Lorna said. *"Please* be careful."

"I'll be careful," Mannering promised, and as he rang off he added mentally: I doubt if there's ever been more need to be.

He turned as he heard a deep voice calling his own name.

"John Mannering? Are you sure?" There was a tap at the door and as Mannering stood up, it opened. There was something both robust and reassuring about the appearance of the tall, powerful-looking man in the dark suit who came in, right hand outstretched.

"Mr. Mannering, I surely am glad to see you! I'm Steven Marshall. I'm sorry I wasn't here when you arrived. If there is anything at all I can do for you —" he broke off, expectantly.

Mannering said: "You're very good. If you could get someone to reserve me a flight to Chicago as soon as possible, I —"

"Why, sure. Irv!" Steven Marshall called. "Will you find out when Flight 307 is leaving—last time I heard it was half-an-hour late. Get Mr. Mannering a seat on it." Marshall turned back to Mannering. "But I hope you'll come back for the opening, sir!"

Mannering chuckled.

"I'm beginning to understand what they mean about Texans! By the way, have you an agent in Chicago, named Ricardi?"

"We sure have," answered Marshall. "Did you meet him?"

"Briefly. He —"

"He has a big cattle outfit in Texas and stockyards in Chicago," Marshall went on, "and he's as enthusiastic about HemisFair as I am. He was to talk to Professor Alundo and finalise the plans for the Professor's lecture." As he spoke, Steven Marshall gave the impression that he was asking questions. This one seemed to be: "Do you know the Professor?"

Mannering said : "I was told Alundo was coming to lecture here. Do you mind telling me why?"

"Sure I'll tell you why. He's a world figure, Mr. Mannering. He fights for what he believes. He gets shouted down too often, so we're giving him a platform in Texas where he won't be shouted down." The new unspoken question was: "Do you object?"

"Can't think of better reasons," Mannering remarked. "Do you know the Professor?"

"No, sir. Ricky went over to England and made all the arrangements last year. He came back with the contract signed—and a very soft spot for the Professor's daughter." Marshall chuckled. "If the Professor doesn't bring her, Ricky will never forgive him."

Mannering finished his dinner, and sat back in his first class seat in a Boeing 727, glancing through brochures on HemisFair, amused by and grateful for Steven Marshall's ready help. He had satisfied himself that Marshall knew of no undercurrents, but was sure he had set the man thinking —particularly when he had asked about Mario Ballas.

"Sure, I know him," Marshall had said. "He has a fine old Mexican house, called La Racienda, fifty or sixty miles into Mexico. In Mexico, he's a good citizen, and who are we to hold what he did in Chicago against him?" When Mannering hadn't answered, the Texan had continued : "I wouldn't condone any crime, Mr. Mannering, but in Mexico, Ballas is looked on as a saint. He's done a great deal to help the poor there, he gives a lot of employment. And"— Marshall gave an infectious grin—"he is exhibiting some rare Mayan art and some early Spanish arms and regalia at HemisFair. Do you object to sharing part of the Jewel House with him?"

Mannering had laughed.

"No more than I would object to selling him anything he wanted."

"We understand each other," Marshall said with satisfaction. "Is there anything else I can do for you?"

"Yes," said Mannering, "I would like some Western-style clothes, and a pocket tape-recorder."

"There's a store right close by the airport," Steven Marshall had said, as if Mannering's were an everyday request. "And I can supply the bugging outfit. Let's go."

That had been three hours ago. The aircraft was now flying over St. Louis and before long the lights of Chicago would be in sight. In less than two hours, Mannering would be in the city.

He was clear in his mind about what he should do.

CHAPTER FIFTEEN

Break-In

MANNERING stood by the corner of Michigan Avenue near the Conrad Hilton, watching the floodlit Planetarium and the museum, seeing the bright headlights of the cars coming towards him from Lakeshore Drive, the brilliant red of those which disappeared over the road across the railway. The hum of traffic, the occasional clatter of footsteps and murmur of voices, were his only company. He walked briskly towards State Street and stood in a doorway, making sure he hadn't been followed. The elongated lamps in their harsh cement posts spread a glow brightened by flashing multi-coloured neon. Here, hundreds walked and buses whined and taxis and cars passed harshly. He saw a taxi with its hire sign alight, and hailed it.

"Do you know where Lake View Apartments are?" he asked. No one would have dreamed from his voice that he was English.

"Yeh."

"Take me there."

The entrance to the apartment building was brightly lit but the street lamps were dim. The taxi stopped. No one appeared to be watching. Mannering stepped out and handed the driver a dollar bill.

No one paid him any attention.

He had booked into the Palmer House Hotel as soon as he had reached Chicago, and had changed into the Western-style clothes he had bought in San Antonio—a wide-brimmed hat, narrow, fancy jeans, and a cowboy shirt of trimmed leather. Unless they examined his face very closely, no one would have suspected this to be the immaculately dressed Englishman known as the Baron.

Now, adopting a rolling-cowboy gait, Mannering strolled to the front entrance of Lake View Apartments. Two men stood just inside the door; he judged them to be either Ballas's men or police, he could not be sure which, but so far as he was concerned it made little difference. He went straight to the elevator, closely watched by the two men, and pressed the penthouse button: PH. The doors opened. As he was taken smoothly upwards, his mind, brilliant, pains-taking, plodding, reviewed for the hundredth time Alundo's desperation to retrieve the microfilm, Ballas's ultimatum, Ethel's disappearance and Ricardi's flight to La Racienda.

The elevator stopped.

Mannering got out, and waited near the elevator shaft for three or four minutes. No one else came up; there was no noise. He walked towards the end of the passage which led to the penthouse. As always, there was a service door to the roof marked with a glowing EXIT in red. He opened this, and stepped on to the narrow ledge between the pent-house walls and the side of the building. The ledge was protected by a waist-high wall which he had seen from the street. He judged the position of Ricardi's flat on the floor below, by comparing it with the street.

He was immediately above the sitting-room window.

He looked over the ledge, very intently. Heights did not worry him but he did not want to take a single unnecessary risk. The ground was a long way down, and it was a sheer drop. He studied the masonry where it jutted, but there was very little to offer in the way of foothold. At this height, eighteen storeys up, all trucks, cars and people below looked minute to the point of distortion.

He could almost hear Alundo's voice again, as he had heard it the second time he had called him.

"There are men outside the apartment, Mannering." And a moment later : "There are men at the emergency exit door."

Men.

Policemen or Ballas's men made no difference for the moment, Mannering decided. Either were likely to stop him from seeing Alundo, and he wanted urgently to talk to the Professor without anyone knowing.

He hitched up his shirt, and unwound from his waist a rope of thin, strong nylon. There were knots in it, and at one end a loop. He placed the loop over a rail, and tightened it, then made a loop at the other end, and slipped it round his waist. Two cars passed, followed by a police car, which drew up outside the building; one of the men inside got out and entered the lobby. He was there for four or five minutes before he climbed back into the car.

Police, thought Mannering, probably waiting for the suspect for the murder of Enrico Ballas. How long ago that seemed ! And how far away La Racienda and San Antonio ! Distance, of time and space, leant to them the unreality of a dream—but there was nothing dreamlike about Ballas or about Steven Marshall.

The police car moved off and the noise of its engine faded. Mannering climbed over the parapet.

Gripping the rope above one of the knots, he gradually eased himself downwards, bracing himself by pushing his feet against the wall. If anyone looked up, he might be seen; but there was a fair chance he would be hidden by the corner-stones and window-ledges.

There was a light in Ricardi's sitting-room.

Mannering went down very slowly, until he was opposite the room. The venetian blinds were half-drawn, but he could see through the slats. All doubts dissolved when he saw Alundo poring over a desk. Mannering lowered himself still farther, and made sure no one else was in the room. At last his feet touched the window ledge.

He could knock and warn Alundo, who would surely let him in, but he preferred complete surprise. First-hand knowledge of the old man's reactions to an emergency would be useful to him. So, gripping the edge of the window frame, he waited. Soon, Alundo got up, without glancing at the window, and went out. Mannering took his tools from his pocket, and worked on the window. At this height they were usually simple. This was a sliding affair with a straightforward catch, which was unlocked. All he had to do was force it to one side. Prising gently with a screwdriver, he made room for the tips of his fingers, then pushed one half behind the other. It made a sharp squeak; that was all.

Mannering wriggled out of the rope, and climbed inside.

Nothing suggested that Alundo had been alarmed, and Mannering walked about, easing his cramped legs and flexing his arms. When he heard the man coming back, he switched on the microphone hanging round his neck, and moved swiftly behind the door.

Alundo came into the room slowly. His face was pale, his grey hair ruffled. As if making a conscious effort, he sat down and picked up the papers he had been studying. Mannering moved forward. The sheets were typewritten, but too far away for him to make sense of them. He crept nearer, until he was able to read over Alundo's shoulder.

Notes for San Antonio Speech.

At the head was the word MISTAKES. The paragraphs beyond this were in smaller typeface. Halfway down was the word ADDITIONS, and near the bottom of the page EMPHASISE. There seemed little doubt that these really were lecture notes, and that Alundo wanted to make the HemisFair lecture foolproof, but—how did this square with a man who was supposed to be almost frantic about his daughter; a man about to trade a deadly secret with a foreign power?

Alundo turned a page.

"More mistakes?" Mannering inquired.

Alundo started so violently that several papers fell to the floor. He did nothing to save them, simply twisted round in his seat, stunned by surprise.

Mannering bent to pick them up. "First mistake—to lie to me," he observed, handing them back to Alundo. "Why didn't you tell me your daughter knew Ricardi in England?"

Alundo seemed too shocked to utter a word.

"Second mistake—to pretend you're a man of peace when in fact you don't care whether Communism wins by peaceful means *or* by war."

Alundo's lips began to work.

"Mannering! Is it—is it *you*?" His incredulous glance roved over the fancy jeans.

"*Are* you a Red—or are you just playing one side against the other?" demanded Mannering, ignoring his question. "If there's one thing I can't stand, it's a man who will sell out his country, for —"

Strength flowed back into Alundo, and he leapt up, incredulity forgotten, fists flying like a furious little boy who could think of nothing else but striking out. And although Mannering fended him off easily enough, he came on again and again, his blows falling inaccurately and without skill.

Hoarse with rage, his voice rose and fell with sobbing persistence :

"Call *me* a traitor!—all I want is *peace*—you imbecile, I don't want money—my God, only a man *soaked* in money would dare to think —" He kept on and on, the words echoing and re-echoing, sometimes audible, sometimes incoherent. Finally spent, his strength ebbing, he drew back, as pallid now as Mario Ballas. Words, however, still poured from him in a voice so muffled that Mannering feared the microphone might miss them.

"You *must* be a fool. I've spent all my life, seeking *peace*. Do you know what peace is? I'll tell you. It's freedom from fear and freedom from want. It's the freedom to say what you like and do what you like without being afraid someone will blow you to pieces or kill you with radiation. *My God!* Have you ever been to Japan? Have you seen what radiation can do? Do you know what would happen to the world if there was a nuclear explosion?"

When he paused, his breathing sounded as if he were gasping for breath, but he would not stop for long.

"Me, a traitor? I've devoted my whole life to England. I've tried to make English people become the hope of the world, but now—look at us. *Look at us.* At the mercy of two great powers, neither of them capable of winning peace. If America could win it, I'd do everything, *everything*, to help. And I'd help Russia, as God's in His heaven I would do everything to help Russia, *if* I thought she wanted world peace. *If.* Oh, she'll *say* she does. Like America, she'll *say* she wants peace. But they both mean the same thing. They mean they want peace if *their* country is top dog. Do you know what happens when there's a top dog? Some other dog waits and waits until there's a chance to spring and pull the top dog down.

"It means war, war, hideous bloody war! But if *I* can help it"—he almost choked—"there won't be any war. I think I can stop it. Given half-a-dozen men of goodwill, I *know* I can. Because what I've discovered is a weapon too fearful for anyone to use. I've got it, Mannering. I've got —"

He broke off, choking again. For a moment Mannering thought he was going to stop breathing. Slowly, gaspingly, he went on:

"Or I did have it, until it was stolen from me. If you know where it is, find it and give it to me. Do you understand? Find and give me the microfilm. *It holds a secret which can destroy all the people in the world.*"

Sweat ran down his forehead. There was a beading of it on his upper lip and about his neck. His lips were aquiver, his whole body ashake, and slowly, as if wearily, he wiped his face.

Gently, Mannering asked : "And if you had it, what would you do with it?"

"That—that is *my* business."

"You will never get that microfilm unless you tell me," Mannering said.

"It's my business ! It —"

"What would you do with it?" Mannering insisted. "What have you been planning? Is it so important that you've even forgotten that your daughter is in danger?"

Alundo seemed to pull up in his tracks, and a look of horror spread over his face. His lips moved after a few seconds, forming a word which he did not utter, but soon Mannering could just hear him whispering *"Ethel. Ethel. Ethel."* His eyes glistened with tears, and he raised his hands towards Mannering as if in supplication.

"Where—where is she, Mannering? Have you—have you found her?"

"Mario Ballas says that he has her," Mannering said flatly. "He wants to exchange her for the microfilm."

Alundo stared at him blankly. "Ballas? That gangster? Oh my poor, poor Ethel." He turned away, pressing a hand to his forehead, as if fighting a stupendous battle within himself. Then, suddenly, he swung back to face Mannering.

"It isn't—it isn't possible," he cried hoarsely. "Even if you *do* find the film, you mustn't do it, Mannering. Do you understand? You—must—not—do—this—thing."

"Professor," Mannering said, "she is your daughter."

"She is—my only child."

"Ballas is a man quite capable of killing her."

"Oh yes. Yes, I know. He may well kill her."

"Professor —"

"Why don't you listen to me?" Alundo cried. There was a new strength in his voice, and a ring of true authority, too. "You must not make the exchange. Should you find the film, you must not let that man have it."

"And your own daughter —"

"Oh, you fool, you ten thousand times a fool! What shall it profit a man if he should save his own flesh and blood and spill the blood of millions? If Ethel has to be sacrificed, or you, or I—then it must be so, but that film must not fall into Mario Ballas's hands. *Do you hear me?*" The old man's voice rang out now, as if he were a prophet declaiming the dangers of hell. "Whatever the cost, whatever the sacrifice, he must not get it."

So Alundo didn't know that Ballas already *had* a copy of the film, thought Mannering. And neither Ballas nor Alundo knew that he, Mannering, had Alundo's copy. Into the strange silence which followed, he asked: "Why not, Alundo?"

"If you knew the man, you would not have to ask. He is evil incarnate. I tell you he is —" Alundo raised his clenched hands, his eyes afire, his voice quivering with passion. *"He is the most evil man in the world."*

As he spoke, another voice rang in Mannering's inner ear, a voice as strained with emotion, as thick with barely controlled rage, as that of Alundo. It was almost as if Alundo's words were a direct echo of those uttered by Ballas.

Mannering frowned; then shrugged the thought away.

"He is a gangster, yes. And he will not, I imagine, be over-kind to Ethel."

Once again Alundo's face showed signs of inner turmoil. And once again, or so it seemed to Mannering, watching him closely, he fought and won (or lost, wondered Mannering) some secret conflict within himself.

For several moments neither man spoke. Then Alundo looked levelly at Mannering. His eyes, at first expressionless, took on a new intensity.

"This means that it *wasn't* one of Ballas's men who stole the briefcase. I thought at first it might have been—especially after what happened on the train. But Ricardi told me —"

"Ricardi," Mannering interrupted him. "How long have you known Ricardi?"

"From the first time I gave the Peace Lecture, in Dallas, eighteen months ago," Alundo said. "He was one of the few who understood, who put his money, his influence, his intelligence, at my disposal. If there were a thousand more like him, what a nation of idealists this country would be!"

What would Alundo say if he knew that Ricardi had been admitted into Ballas's hideaway so freely?

"We can use idealists," Mannering said dryly, and then asked abruptly: "What's this talk you're to give to San Antonio? And when is it?"

"It is a week tomorrow," answered Alundo. "And it will be my Peace Prize Lecture."

"How is it you can give a peace lecture at a World Fair?"

"It is a better place than most," the old man said. "My Peace Prize Lecture was honoured, two years ago, although the world has forgotten. Last year's winner is sick, this year's winner died two months ago, so—I am to speak. And when I speak—Mannering! Listen to me. When I speak I want to tell the world that *I have destroyed that microfilm.* That is why I must have it. If you have any heart, if you have any conscience, if you have any love for mankind, find the film and give it to me.

"If you do not—the curse of all mankind be on your head."

CHAPTER SIXTEEN

The Curse . . .

"THE curse of all mankind be on your head."

The words echoed and re-echoed in Mannering's mind as he watched Alundo. As they came out, the man had seemed afire, but the flame slowly died, the light faded from his eyes, his body sagged. He backed a pace and dropped on to the couch, almost in a state of collapse. Suddenly he looked very, very old. Mannering crossed to a small bar, poured out a brandy and brought it to him. The Professor's hand quivered as he drank. Finished, he said in a voice which was hardly audible:

"What's the use? What *is* the use?" He shook his head, wearily. "No one ever listens. No one really cares. If I was to shout from the housetops that the world was coming to an end, no one would pause to listen. Unless I have something to *prove* what I say in the Peace Lecture, no one will listen. The audience will nod and doze and wake up to applaud, and then drop off again. The politicians talk only in asinine platitudes. Sometimes I think all *I* talk are platitudes."

"Think again, now you've got all that off your chest," Mannering said. "What do you want most? Your daughter's safety, or the microfilm."

Alundo's eyes took on a little of their former fire.

"I have no choice," he said. "The film is *all* important." Then he added: "I haven't really a chance, have I? *You* don't know where —"

Mannering said: "How long have you been working for peace?"

"Most of my life," answered Alundo, with a proud lift of his head.

"How often have you given up hope?"

Frowning, the old man answered : "Never."

"Why give it up now?"

"I am an old man, Mannering."

"With less time than a young one, and so more need of faith. What were you doing when I came in?"

"I was revising notes for my lecture."

"Why don't you go on revising them?" Mannering said. "You've nearly eight days."

Alundo blinked at him, frowned again, then clasped his hands together very firmly. He did not speak. After a long time, he nodded. A curious transformation came on his lined face, a kind of peacefulness. Finally, he smiled, and turned away. He was holding his notes, and putting on a pair of thick-lensed glasses, when suddenly he said, in alarm:

"Mr. Mannering!"

"Yes?"

"The police are looking for you."

"Yes, I know."

"But they're outside—outside this very door."

"I daresay they are."

"Then how did you get in?"

Mannering smiled. "Perhaps it's as well we don't know everything. Exactly what happened to Ethel?"

"She—she went off, early this morning."

"Did she say where she was going?"

"I understood—I understood she was going to look for you. Ricardi has gone to find her, but I have heard nothing from him."

"Did he know there was danger from Ballas?"

"Yes, yes," said Alundo. He fiddled with his glasses. "It was from Ricardi that I learned that the danger did come from Ballas. There were interruptions at my lecture in

Chicago, and Ricardi traced the source—men paid by Ballas to discredit me. And it has gone on and on. At some of my lectures there have been hooligans who have interrupted, shouted me down. Some of the newspapers have been full of bitter attacks on me. Ballas owns some of these newspapers and can influence others. I tell you, he is evil incarnate."

"Do you trust Ricardi?"

Very slowly, Alundo said: "I do not trust anyone, not even my own daughter. It is a time of false ideologies. The poison of nationalism and the poison of Communism are equally virulent. Families are divided by them, husbands and wives are split asunder. Until there can be trust again, there can be no hope of peace."

"You trusted Ethel to bring the package over."

"In moments of crisis one is sometimes forced to take dangerous risks to escape those of a greater danger. I had intended to go back myself but I was too closely followed. Whenever I went to a public call box, men came up to me and I—I was frightened. There was no time to write—no certainty that a letter would reach her. I was not even sure that my telephone call was untapped, and—certainly it was discovered that Ethel brought the film here —"

"Who knew?"

"If my line was tapped, anyone could have known."

"If it wasn't?"

Alundo gulped, but did not hesitate.

"Ricardi."

"Only Ricardi?"

"Yes," Alundo assured him. "There could have been no one else. He has greatly admired Ethel for months. Even while she was in England he talked about her a great deal. He has several photographs of her. We—we do not always see eye-to-eye and she does not share my—my passionate views. But after all, she is my only child. We have not always got on very well, she is impetuous and imperious, so like her mother. And no doubt I am old and stubborn. Ethel has no patience with my attempts to put the world right, she thinks one should live for oneself alone."

"I see," said Mannering, and then asked casually:

"How well do you know Lord Fentham?"

In surprise, Alundo answered: "Very well indeed, he is one of the financial sponsors of my tour—a great man, a very great man. What made you ask?"

"Did he know you were in trouble?"

"He did indeed."

"Does he know of the microfilm?"

Alundo said wearily: "There is no point in prevaricating. Yes, he knows. He is one of the few true workers for peace."

"There may be more than you realise," Mannering said. "Couldn't you trust *him*?"

"I most certainly could," said Alundo. "He is the only man I could trust. But these wicked men know of his friend-ship. To have asked him would have put him in deadly danger, whereas my daughter would not—should not—have been suspected. For her to visit me would seem quite nor-mal."

"I suppose you're right," Mannering said, and went on abruptly: "I'm going now. You —"

The telephone bell rang across his words. Alundo seemed to shrink back as if fearful. Mannering turned, picked up the receiver slowly, put a finger against his lips for silence, and spoke into the mouthpiece.

No one would have recognised him.

As quickly as he had acquired an American accent, now he spoke in Alundo's voice—that rather high-pitched, slightly querulous tone.

"Yes? Who is it?"

"Pro—Professor," a man said huskily. "Professor, they —"

"Who is that? Speak up, please."

"Its—Ricky," the other said, like a man in great pain. "They—won't—they won't let her go without the —"

Mannering broke in, still querulous but very anxious now.

"Are you all right, Ricky? Where —"

"They—they—they beat me up," Ricardi answered. "And they flew me right back to Ballas's private runway. I—I'm at one of the Lakeshore parks. In a call-box. Near the Planetarium." He paused. "They pushed me out of a car. They won't let Ethel go, unless you —"

"Listen to me," Mannering said. "Wait there. I will —"

"Don't come to me," Ricardi said urgently. "Don't take risks, Professor. But—it's Ethel or the microfilm. Don't make any mistake."

He rang off. Alundo, hardly crediting his own ears, sat staring at him. Mannering put the receiver down quickly.

"That was Ricardi. He didn't have any luck."

"I knew that he had no chance, I warned him. Is he all right?"

"He's alive," Mannering said heavily. "How many policemen are outside?"

"Two."

"I want you to call them in," Mannering said. "Tell them you heard something in the back room, and you want them to search it."

He did not plead or argue, and he did not doubt that Alundo would obey.

Two minutes later he stood by the open door of a clothes closet, hearing the two men come in, then hearing Alundo's scared voice. He waited until voices and footsteps faded into the back room, went to the front door and peered out into the passage. No one was in sight. He went down two flights of stairs, then took the elevator to the second floor, got out and walked down the last flight of stairs. He glanced into the hall and saw the doorman talking to a thickset policeman who was stifling a yawn. He went out of the side door towards the car park, then along towards the main highway. Two taxis passed. He beckoned the third, and said:

"Take me to the nearest car rental office, will you?"

Twenty minutes later he was driving a Chevrolet along Lakeshore Drive. Every now and again there was a turn off to a bathing station and wooded park, and at each he stopped, got out of the car, and called "Ricardi". There was no answer. At the fourth, he thought he heard a muffled cry, and taking a pencil-thin torch from his pocket, he flashed it across the ground. Its beam fell at last on the huddled figure of a man. Mannering shone the torchlight over his face—and it showed crimson.

He caught his breath as he felt the other's limbs firmly but carefully, passing his hand gently over the back of his head. As he laid him carefully back on to the ground, he heard a chink—and looking down, saw Ricardi's key-ring, which had fallen from his pocket. Mannering picked it up, hesitated, then slipped it into his own pocket. Then he went to the booth, dialled the operator, and said in his American voice:

"There's a man lying near this telephone—Lakeside 8–1001. He's taken a hell of a beating, he needs an ambulance real bad."

"I'll connect you with the police, sir, if —"

"You tell the cops, I don't want any part of it." Mannering replaced the receiver, got back into the Chevrolet, and waited. At last he heard the siren of an ambulance or a police car, and soon lights turned towards the call-box. He stayed long enough to see the vehicle stop and men get out, then he drove off.

He had a few minutes to think.

Now he had to face the fact that Ethel was a captive of Ballas, in Mexico, and that Ballas was still prepared to have a man viciously beaten up. He had two stories to reconcile, and was quite convinced that the secret of the microfilm in the locker at the Conrad Hilton was—deadly.

Deadly?

The word actually made him laugh.

Could it all be true? Or was it conceivable that both Alundo and Ballas had been fooled?

The only way to begin to find out was to get the packet. But supposing he ran the gauntlet of the police and Ballas's men at the hotel, what good would it do him? He could study the film, he could even project it, but how could he be sure that it was genuine?

He smiled wryly as he turned into another of the parks, where the light of a telephone booth glowed. He pulled up, then walked back to the booth, jingling coins in his pocket. He opened the telephone directory, and ran his forefinger down the H's to Hennessy, found Hennessy, D.R.R., K.C.V.O., and dialled a Murray Hill number. The ringing sound went on for a long time.

A man answered at last.

"This is Sir Donald Hennessy's residence."

"Tell him Mr. Toby Plender would like a word with him," Mannering said.

"Is it business, sir? Or personal? Sir Donald is at a meeting, and —"

"Highly personal, highly business and extremely urgent," Mannering said.

He waited, heart thumping, wondering whether the message would reach Hennessy. Soon there were clicks on the line and a deep, resonant voice sounded with obvious pleasure.

"Why, Toby! I'd no idea you were in Chicago!"

"He's not," said Mannering. "I am."

There was a brief pause, before Hennessy said: "Who is that —" He broke off. "John!"

"Hallo, Donald," Mannering said. "Surprised?"

"*Surprised?* That's putting it mildly. My God, man, all the police in Chicago are looking for you!"

"That's my problem," Mannering said lightly. "They won't believe the story of my innocence until it's too late. Donald —"

"Why the deuce don't you give yourself up?" demanded Hennessy.

"The evidence against me is too strong."

"But in heaven's name —"

"Let me get a word in edgeways," Mannering pleaded. "I want a simple piece of information which you may be able to give me."

"If I can I will," promised Hennessy. "But I still think— oh, what is it?"

"Has there been a major leak of a supremely important new weapon?" asked Mannering, quietly.

"Wh —" Hennessy began, then broke off. He kept silent for a long time, while Mannering grew restless. Then in a calmer and more reasonable voice than he had yet used, he went on: "Yes. A discovery was made by two research physicists working for a commercial company. Both men were murdered—but one left a letter saying that two microfilms had been made of the discovery and the experiments leading up to it—both microfilms are now missing." He paused. "John, what do *you* know about all this?"

"I might have one of the microfilms," Mannering said.

"*What!*"

"Unintentionally," Mannering explained hastily.

"Is it *safe*?"

"For the time being, yes. Donald, listen, I need free passage into the Conrad Hilton Hotel and protection by the police from some men working for Mario Ballas —"

"My God," breathed Hennessy. "Do you want to get yourself killed three ways?"

"And I want someone to take this microfilm and give me

a replacement that looks exactly like it—and I want it by tomorrow morning."

"How in heaven's name do you expect me to fix a thing like that?"

"You can do it," Mannering said. "One condition."

"*You're* in no position to make conditions!"

"I want freedom of movement in and out of Chicago for at least a week."

After another pause, Hennessy said : "If it's the real thing, John, you'd deserve that, even if you'd killed a dozen Ballas's. Where are you?"

"I'll call you every half-hour, on the half-hour," Mannering promised. "Don't let me down."

He called five times, from five different call-boxes.

Each time, his heart beat very fast, at near suffocation point, he was so affected by the tension.

It was not until the sixth call that he heard the welcome words : "Sir Donald would like to speak to you now, sir. Please hold on."

CHAPTER SEVENTEEN

Catastrophic

"John," Hennessy said, "we know that two copies of those films existed. You've just told me that you think Ballas has one copy; and that Alundo had the other but that you removed it from Ethel Alundo's briefcase and put it in a locker at the Conrad Hilton. Enough is known about the nature of this discovery to enable the experts to check if the film you have is genuine. And it's on an Italian film seldom used in England."

"Good," said Mannering. "You'll be able to prove that I'm not lying. Where can it be checked?"

"Here in Chicago. An F.B.I. team and two of the War Department experts are on their way from Washington. Where will you meet them?"

"Am I free to move about?"

"The hounds are off you, but tell me where you are, and you'll be looked after."

"Donald," Mannering said, "this isn't so simple, and I can't explain why. I want to meet the F.B.I. team where it's impossible for me to be followed without knowing it."

"Where?"

"Why not a station on the elevated?"

"Why not? Which station?"

"Chicago Avenue. If they wear a red flower in the left lapel and carry a newspaper in their right hand, I'll recognise them."

"At ten o'clock," Hennessy promised. "What are you going to do meanwhile?"

"Eat."

"For God's sake be careful."

"I'll be careful," Mannering said. "Thanks, Donald."

He put down the receiver and stepped out of the box. The pale glow of his watch dial showed eight-thirty. He got into the car and drove downtown, watching the lights of every car behind him. None followed—of course none followed, who would possibly recognise him? Yet he was on edge. He turned into a car parking lot on a corner of State Street, with the great girders of the elevated railway and the huge pillars supporting them overhead. A train rumbled above. The sound was deafening, but dozens of people walked by as if they did not hear it. Getting out of the car, he strolled along the brightly lit street, one of hundreds but still very watchful. Now and again he had a mental picture of Ricardi in his mind's eye. Poor devil.

What kind of a man had Ballas become? And what had possessed him, Mannering, almost to warm to the man?

He turned in to a drug store, bright with neon lighting, filled with cheap goods. The pharmaceutical section was at one end, a long soda fountain bar along one side. He bought some simple make-up accessories, as if a present for a woman, and went. out. Next he bought a postcard of the Planetarium, begged an envelope, and wrote on the post-card :

If I'm prevented from keeping my appointment ask the Room Clerk at the Conrad Hilton for the key given to him by Mr. Mendelsohn. It is for a locker in the lower lobby.

He signed this with his own name, and sealed the envelope, addressing it to the Chief of Police, Chicago, then pushed it quickly into a posting box. Seeing a men's room, he slipped unobtrusively inside, unwrapped the make-up he had just purchased, and worked steadily on his face for twenty minutes. He was still wearing the Western-style clothes—and when he had finished with the make-up, John Mannering, to all outward appearances, had disappeared.

Still checking carefully that no one followed him, he left the drug-store, and turned in to a restaurant with a charcoal fire glowing in the window and half a dozen steaks sizzling on the bars. A huge notice read STEAK DINNER ONE DOLLAR NINETY-FIVE CENTS. ALL YOU CAN EAT. He had a table for four to himself. A pert waitress put a double portion of butter into his baked Idaho potato, hovering invitingly as she refilled his coffee cup. The steak was good, but he made himself eat slowly.

At five minutes to ten, he walked up the iron steps to the station. A dozen people were standing about, forlornly. No one who might be his men were there. He stood at a corner of the shelter, then, as he waited, saw first one, then another well-dressed man appear. Each had a red carnation in his left lapel, each carried a newspaper in his right hand. So far, so good. Mannering made no move towards them as they began to walk to and fro, showing no interest in him or in anybody.

Caution warned : wait.

Mannering waited.

And as he waited, two more men appeared. One of them, looming massive and brutal in the poor light of the station, was Tiger O'Leary.

It was useless to ask *how* Ballas's men came to be here; they were an ever-present threat. It was obvious that Ballas ran a kind of ferry service between La Racienda and Chicago, and as obvious that O'Leary would like nothing better than to kill him, Mannering.

If there were two of Ballas's men, would there be others?

As Mannering waited, listening to the growing roar of an

approaching train, O'Leary passed within a yard of him. Mannering was more than ever aware of Ricardi as he had last seen him, his face bloody and battered. The train roared nearer, blaring into sight, great headlight blazing. Mannering walked towards the platform edge, as if ready to board the train. He had a sense of great urgency; a sense that every second counted. He stood within a foot or two of O'Leary, knowing the man was waiting for the passengers to alight, his whole attention diverted from those round him. The train ground to a standstill. Suddenly, unexpectedly, he swung round on O'Leary for the second time, and brought his knee up into the pit of the man's stomach. O'Leary gasped. His eyes rolled and he collapsed on to the platform, but his companion's right hand flew upwards, moving towards the gun in his shoulder holster. Mannering struck him beneath the chin, hard enough to lift him off his feet and rock him against the side of the train. A few people were jumping off, others were getting in, no one but the F.B.I. men appeared to see what was happening. Mannering spun round towards them.

"They came from Ballas," he said, distinctly. "Catch me up—I'll be in the drug store across the road."

He turned and ran down the steps, footsteps clattering, still not sure that there *was* none of Ballas's men on the other side of the track. The train began to move out, drowning the sounds he made. He raced across the street through a gap in the traffic, and into the doorway of the drug store. Two or three people watched him curiously, but no one showed any active interest. Almost at once, the two men with the red carnations appeared. They were held up by a stream of traffic, but no one followed them down the steps.

Mannering waited for them to cross. The first one touched the kerb, saying:

"Get in the Buick." He pointed.

A black sedan stood just round the corner, a driver at the

wheel. Mannering reached it a few yards ahead of the two men, turned to watch the station, was reassured, and got in. The others almost fell on top of him, and the car moved before the door was closed.

"Nice to know you can hurry," Mannering said.

One of the others eased himself into a more comfortable position before saying grimly :

"What's got into you, Mr. Mannering?"

"Ballas's man, O'Leary," Mannering said. "I'd met him before."

"Why didn't he recognise you on the station?"

"He recognised *you*."

"*What?*"

"Must have, Ken," interpolated the second man. He was very thickset, with heavy features relieved by a smile which played about his lips all the time. The other man was taller, thinner, grimmer. The peak of his hat pushed back, showing a frontal baldness. "We were picked up and followed."

The man named Ken asked: "Did he come on to the station behind us?"

Mannering nodded.

"Don't fight the odds, Ken," the shorter man said. "We led them to Mannering and Mannering led us away. Glad to know you, Mr. Mannering."

"Do you think we can feel safe now?" Mannering asked gruffly.

"No one followed, and this time we were looking."

"Where do we go?" asked the man named Ken.

"Gentlemen," Mannering said, "may I see your identification papers, please?"

Ken, the lean one, stared then broke into a laugh. Each man took out a card. The tall man was Kennedy J. Silver, the short one Piet Vandorn. Each had a photograph attached to the card which was signed by J. Edgar Hoover. As they tucked them away, Mannering said:

"You go to the Conrad Hilton, and . . ." He told them how to get the manuscript. "How long will it take to check the film?"

"Maybe two hours."

"What I would like to do is go to my hotel room and sleep," Mannering said. "I've a lot to catch up. But not the Conrad Hilton—one of Ballas's men may have been there. I've booked in at the Palmer House."

Ten minutes later, the F.B.I. men walked out of the Conrad Hilton and stepped into the car, Ken carrying the manuscript. He handed this to Mannering, who ruffled through it, feeling a momentary panic lest the strips of microfilm had disappeared. But they were still there.

With a sigh of relief he handed it over.

"Don't lose it."

"We won't lose it, and we won't lose you," Ken said. "You're coming with us, Mannering."

"Don't be silly," Mannering said.

"We're not going to let you out of our sight."

"Do you ever want to get Mario Ballas and *his* copy of the film?" Mannering asked heavily, "or do you like him where he is?" When neither of the others answered, he said: "If Ballas knows there's been a switch of Alundo's film, I won't have a chance to see him again. If he thinks I've still got it and will deal with him, he'll make the deal. And when he's made it, he'll either cut my throat, or release me. If he releases me, I'll report to you. In either case, get the Mexican police to raid him and find the film already in his possession." He paused for a moment, then added: "Didn't Sir Donald tell you the conditions?"

"He told us," Ken said.

"There's one thing you forget," said Vandorn.

"I didn't kill Enrico Ballas, if that's what you mean."

"We're not worried about Enrico Ballas at this stage. We want you alive."

"I'm alive."

"At the moment; but we'd like you to stay that way. You'll never get into the Ballas house and escape a second time."

Mannering said: "There's always a risk."

"This is a thousand-to-one against risk."

"*You* don't have to take it," Mannering said. "*I'm* taking it."

Piet Vandorn said quietly: "Why should you, Mannering? Why stick your neck out?"

"What's in this for you?" Ken asked, cynicism redolent in his voice.

Mannering leaned back in the car and closed his eyes, then said almost wearily:

"You should first hear what Alundo has to say. And you should then hear what Ballas had to say. Each in his own way thinks the end of the world is coming. For myself, perhaps I think the same thing, but in a different form and a different kind of world. In my world, a man does his job because it's his job. I'm a dealer in *objets d'art* and precious stones. *And* I'm a consultant—what you call a private eye. I've dealt for years with Lord Fentham, and when he told me that he'd been robbed of some family jewels and asked me to get them back, I came here to do just that. I think he was robbed by Enrico Ballas, and I think the jewels may be in Mario Ballas's house. I want to find them. And at the same time I want to find out who killed Enrico, because until we know, I'll be under suspicion."

Ken said, acidly: "So you want to save your neck."

"Don't pay any attention to this guy, Mannering," Vandorn said. "I'll fix it."

"Fixing it" took a few minutes by radio.

They drove back to the Palmer House Hotel, and Mannering stripped down to singlet and trunks, and stretched out on the bed. He lay on the verge of sleep, dreaming of all the things which had led him here, the past as well as the present. There wasn't much to add to what he had said to the F.B.I. men.

He was half asleep when the telephone bell at his side rang, and for a moment he did not know what it was. Then he sat up abruptly, and lifted the receiver.

"Hallo."

"John." It was Hennessy, speaking at his most deliberate. "I've news for you."

"Let's have it."

"You will probably be decorated by Washington *and* the Kremlin."

Mannering's heart seemed to turn over, and then beat very fast.

"Did you hear me?" Hennessy asked.

"I—yes, I heard."

"A wonderful job, John."

"Er—it's all right, so far."

"John."

"Yes?"

"Don't go back to Ballas."

"My dear chap —"

"You've done more than enough."

"Not yet, Donald."

"You don't have to be twice a hero."

"I have to know who killed Enrico and I have to know where Fentham's diamonds are."

"I'm begging you not to go ahead, John."

"I'll tell you another thing," Mannering said. "Professor Alundo is preparing his big speech for the United Nations. He'll do a better job if he knows his daughter is safe. She's at La Racienda. Do you think the Mexican police would find her if they went there?"

"No," said Hennessy, heavily. "I don't. And in any case, they'd want a lot of evidence before they *would* raid Ballas. They might do it if you could prove he'd broken Mexican law—or if we told them about the microfilm. But that's the one thing no one must know about. *No one*," repeated Hennessy urgently, "not even for the girl's sake. Once it was common knowledge that such a film existed —" He broke off.

There was a moment's silence—broken, at last, by Mannering.

"You haven't found out how Ricardi is, I suppose?"

"He won't die," Hennessy said gruffly, "but he's still unconscious. Poor fellow. John —"

"You needn't remind me," Mannering said. "Ballas won't be any respecter of persons. Is that fake microfilm ready?"

Hennessy grunted.

"Oh well, if you *must* commit suicide—yes it is. It's on Italian film all right and is good enough to fool anyone except experts. It will be at your hotel inside the hour."

"Thanks. Am I free to move about as I like?"

"Yes."

"And I won't be followed by the police or the F.B.I.?"

"I've been assured not. If you need a police contact in San Antonio, your man is Pollitzer—Captain Pollitzer. He's on good terms with the Mexican police across the border."

"Thanks," Mannering said. After a short silence, he went on: "If things *should* go wrong, tell Lorna I felt I couldn't back out, will you?"

"Yes," Hennessy said heavily. "I'll tell her. But I hope I'll never—oh, the hell with it! Good luck, John!"

"Thanks," Mannering said. "I'll be seeing you."

As he put down the receiver he was already beginning to

plan his tactics for his next visit to Mario Ballas. He was sure of one thing: the simpler and more direct, the better. He could never be more tortuous than Ballas; but he might fool him with simplicity.

The wisest way to start was to sleep and so be at his very best tomorrow.

CHAPTER EIGHTEEN

Simplicity

MANNERING woke, slowly, pleasantly, with no fear on his mind, no weight of apprehension. He rang room service for coffee and toast and mused while he waited, the events of the previous day coming back slowly and vividly, touching his mind with fear, but never raising a doubt of the wisdom and necessity of what he had to do.

By half-past eight on a clear, fresh morning, with a wind blowing off the lake, he walked briskly towards a taxi stand, took a cab to the Planetarium, where so much had started, and then strode along the lakeside, already feeling the warmth of the sun.

By half-past nine, he was entering the Conrad Hilton Hotel.

He collected his key, but saw no one whom he recognised, went up to his room, and cautiously approached the door.

Was it only a day since he had brought Ethel here?

He unlocked the door, opened it an inch—then flung it back. No one was here. He felt a little foolish, but far better be foolish than dead. He thought ruefully that he was getting too old to play this kind of game—Tiger O'Leary was ten or fifteen years younger; the odds would soon be too heavy.

He closed and locked the door, and stood surveying the room. The danger now was from a booby trap. He went through the drawers, the bureau, the cupboards, very deliberately and carefully but found nothing to alarm him. Soon, the only piece left to search was the bed. He pulled back the bedspread, then the one blanket, then the sheet—

and the sheet was only a few inches down when he saw something there.

He stopped, and studied it. It *looked* like the top of a photograph, but a single sheet of paper could be so impregnated with high explosive that it could kill a dozen men.

Would Ballas want him dead—yet?

He edged the sheet down, and was soon satisfied that it was a photograph; the top of a woman's head showed first, then her forehead, then —

It was Ethel.

Still slowly, acutely aware of the booby trap danger, he picked the photograph up. It was an excellent one, and almost certainly taken yesterday; he recognised easily the way her hair was worn, a small cameo brooch at the shoulder. There was nothing written on the front, and Mannering turned it over.

There were three short paragraphs, typewritten, and stuck on to the back, and each was numbered.

1. Your young friend appears to be innocent. She can lay in a great many beds, and lose that innocence. Do you think she would like that?

2. Or she can be mutilated, as Ricardi was mutilated. How much worse for an attractive woman.

3. Or she can retain her virginity and her beauty and forget this nightmare, if you bring me the object I desire. It *must* be genuine, not a fake.

Mannering shivered and closed his eyes. Outside the sun was bright and the morning fair, but this room seemed full of shadows. Resolutely he studied the photograph more closely, then pulled the telephone towards him and, still marvelling, dialled the San Antonio Police Headquarters. He was through as quickly as if it had been a local call.

"Captain Pollitzer, please."

"Yes, sir. Who wants him?"

"John Mannering."

"Yes, sir, Mr. Mannering." Obviously the operator wasn't surprised by the name.

After a moment a man spoke in a voice so deep the words were difficult to understand at first.

"What can I do for you, Mr. Mannering? I hope you've changed your mind!" He wasn't surprised, either.

"No," Mannering said. "I still intend to go to Mexico. And I want to ask you one simple question."

"What is it?"

"What help can I rely on from the San Antonio police?"

"Against Mario Ballas?"

"Yes."

"As much help as you need, if —"

Ah, thought Mannering; the evasion was coming.

". . . if you can make out a *prima facie* case. He is very clever, Mr. Mannering. You won't find it easy, and he will have a dozen men to lie for him, if necessary. Because he is in Mexico it is more difficult. He has a very different reputation there from here. But the San Antonio *and* the Mexican police will help if you can prove the need. Mr. Mannering —"

"Yes?"

"It wouldn't surprise me if Ballas had your telephone tapped."

"Although I dialled direct."

"It's still possible," Pollitzer said. "If you want to talk to me about anything you plan to do, call me from a pay-box."

"Captain Pollitzer."

"Yes?"

"Are you sure *your* telephone isn't tapped?"

Pollitzer gave a rumble of laughter.

"Sure I'm sure," he said. "Will you call me?"

"Yes," Mannering said. "Have you had any word from Chicago about Ricardi this morning?"

"It'll be a very long time before he's up and about again. But he'll live."

"He was really worked over."

"I'll say he was worked over. Mannering —"

"Yes?"

"They can do worse."

"To me—or to Alundo's daughter?"

After a pause, Pollitzer said:

"Everything I ever heard about you seems true, Mannering. I'll be in my office when you call."

He rang off.

Mannering went downstairs to the coffee shop, ordered and ate a fairly substantial meal, then walked to a row of callboxes. Two were vacant. He dialled the police again, inserted the coins he was told to, and was put through to Pollitzer in an instant.

"You found a reason for my breaking into Ballas's house?" Pollitzer demanded.

"Yes."

"It had better be good."

"You want me, remember?" Mannering said. "My photograph is in the *Tribune* and the *Sun*. I'm wanted for murder, and for robbery with violence. I'm a very bad man indeed. If you tell the Mexican police *I'm* at La Racienda, and *Ballas* is in danger —"

Pollitzer interrupted almost softly :

"*Will* you be at Ballas's house?"

"I will be there at six o'clock tonight," Mannering said. "If I'm not out by seven o'cock, will you make plans for me?"

"I certainly will."

"Pulling every string you can," Mannering urged.

"Mr. Mannering," Pollitzer said, "someone has been feeding you stories about the American Police Departments. We want Ballas, and we want him as badly as you do. We'll get him any way we can."

"Thanks," Mannering said.

"Will you call again?" Pollitzer said. "With more details, maybe?"

"No," Mannering answered. "These are all the details you need. Good luck."

"*I* need the luck!" Pollitzer growled.

Mannering rang off, and walked away. No one followed him. He went to the car park where he had left the hired car, and drove to Lake View Apartments. Two men were outside, obviously watching. From Ballas? Or the police? He parked, strode into the lobby, went up alone in the elevator, and approached Ricardi's apartment. He listened at the door, and imagined he could hear men's voices. He selected one of two Yale keys from Ricardi's key-ring, and slipped it silently into the lock. It turned, and the door opened. Mannering pushed the door a few inches, and heard Alundo saying :

". . . supreme importance, absolutely *supreme* importance, Frederick. If I could have produced both films at the crucial moment of my speech—*what* a sensation! *What* a sensation! It would have rung round the world. For the first time in history the secret of one of the great weapons would have been at the disposal of *all* nations."

"H'm. Yes. H'm." In an instant's sharp surprise, Mannering recognised the voice of Freddie Fentham. "Quite true, no doubt. But now *both* films have been stolen —" Fentham paused. "Little enough chance of getting *one* copy back, let alone two."

"I—don't—know." Alundo sounded dispirited, but not so dispirited as Mannering would have expected after his discovery that the second film was also missing. "I think Mannering *may* succeed in finding them. It is certainly a remarkably fortuitous happening that he should be here at this time."

Mannering said dryly : "Not exactly fortuitous, Freddie, is it?"

Alundo spun round. Fentham's mouth dropped open for a moment in complete surprise, but he recovered quickly. He looked tired, but apart from this, as healthy and fit as usual. He wore a suit of grey Harris tweed, as perfect for the Yorkshire moors as it was out of place in a Chicago spring.

"Hallo, John. Forgive me not getting up. I've had a very tiring day. The aircraft was two hours late at Kennedy. How are you?"

"Fine, by the grace of God, and in spite of you, the Professor, and Mario Ballas."

Alundo said excitedly: "My dear Mannering! How on earth did you get in? This is the second time you've appeared out of the air!"

"Walks through blank walls," Fentham said, smiling faintly. "Eh, John? I knew you would be all right. Man of ninety-nine lives."

"I *insist* on knowing what this is about." Alundo was not far from anger.

"I went to see Ricardi last night, and borrowed his keys," Mannering answered easily. "And Fentham virtually compelled me to come to America, but apparently he gave me a false reason."

"Oh, not false, John," Fentham protested. "Additional. To cut a long story short, Alundo had two copies of the microfilm; he kept one, and gave me the other. We thought it would be safer that way. Alundo hid his copy in his lecture notes—I hid mine in the setting of the necklace and bracelet. I telephoned him to say what I'd done, but the line must have been tapped, because a few days later both necklace and bracelet were stolen. I've come over here to tell him what's happened, and now he tells me his copy has been stolen as well."

Mannering ignored his last sentence. "Good Lord! So it was *you* who had the second copy. And *that's* why only the necklace and bracelet were taken and the rest of the collection was left."

"Precisely."

Mannering looked at Freddie bleakly. "And you asked me to find those two pieces without telling me what was hidden inside them; you pitched me into one of the most murderous situations imaginable, without a word of warning!"

"My dear chap, if I'd told you the whole story you might have washed your hands of it from the word go," said Fentham, almost testily. "And I happen to have greater faith in you on this kind of job than in the F.B.I. and M.I.6 and C.I.A. put together. How *are* things at the moment, John?"

"Are you any nearer finding the films?" Alundo demanded.

"A little," Mannering said, almost grudgingly. "I'll have news for you by tonight. Have you heard from Ethel?"

"Not a word." Alundo passed a tired hand across his eyes. "Poor child. She —"

"What's this about Ethel?" asked Fentham sharply.

Mannering told him what had happened, and Fentham stood up and began to pace the room.

"This is very worrying, very worrying indeed. What has Ballas demanded?" Before Mannering could answer, Fentham went on: "Ethel in exchange for the film, I suppose. Pity. *Great* pity you ever brought Ethel over, Arthur, it made you much more vulnerable."

"She was the *only* one apart from you whom I could even half-trust," Alundo said sadly. "Mannering, as I told you yesterday, these stakes are far too high to worry about the fate of individuals. Far too high. Freddie, surely you agree. Can't you persuade Mannering —"

Mannering unrolled the photograph, held it out so that they could see who it was, then turned it over. Both men read it closely.

"John," Fentham said gruffly, when he had finished reading. "I don't like it any more than you do, but an arrangement would be unthinkable."

Mannering allowed his words to pass without comment. "What's your part in all this?" he asked.

"A very simple one," answered Fentham. "I'm interested in the Action for Peace Committee, and one of the judges of the Peace Lecture Award, as you know, and not exactly a poor man. Most of the Peace Movements have been run on a shoestring, but I've thought for years that one might *buy* peace the same way that one buys secrets about war. Then when Arthur heard of this new discovery, he thought it might be possible to do something quite dramatic. Such as announce it to the world and then publicly destroy it. If you can get it back, you will serve the whole of mankind. You really will. Sorry if that sounds sententious : it happens to be true. And that, relatively speaking, is far more important than saving Ethel, no matter what might happen to her."

Mannering saw the aircraft which Ballas had promised to send for him at Fort Worth airport. He recognised Cyrus Lake, and went towards him. It was difficult to understand Cyrus's expression when he said:

"The Boss was the only one who thought you would come back."

"Did you need telling he was a judge of men?" demanded Mannering.

CHAPTER NINETEEN

Terms . . .

BALLAS sat in the golden chair, exactly as he had done before, but this time Cyrus Lake, Tiger O'Leary, and two other men were with him; escape would be quite impossible. Mannering did not stand away from the inlaid desk but placed his hands on it, leaning forward. It was only three hours since the plane had taken off from Fort Worth for La Racienda.

"Condition one : I want to see Ethel Alundo before I say a word about terms," Mannering said.

It was impossible to judge what was passing through Ballas's mind, but almost at once he said to Cyrus Lake :

"Send for her."

"She—she may not be awake."

"Bring her, whether she's awake or not."

Cyrus said : "Sure." He went out but another man stepped in, so that four still remained. Ballas looked tired, his eyes red-rimmed, his face set in an alabaster pallor. Slowly, his lids drooped. Mannering could only just discern the movement at his breast, none at all at his nostrils or lips. They must have sat in that silent stillness for seven or eight minutes before a buzz sounded at the door. Opening his eyes, Ballas touched a different spot from that of the knob Mannering had previously found. The door clicked open, and Cyrus Lake came in with Ethel.

She was awake; just.

Heavy-eyed and sluggish of movement, she showed no outward sign of injury. Her hair was dishevelled and her dress rumpled and creased, as if she had slept in it; there were some red ridges on her right forearm. She moistened her lips.

"I want a drink of water."

"You can have a drink when you've spoken to Mr. Mannering," Ballas said.

She looked at Mannering. Slow recognition dawned in her eyes, but no indication followed that he meant anything to her. Inert, uncaring, the impression she gave was that of a woman only half awake, or drugged.

"Hallo," she said.

"Hallo, Ethel," Mannering said gently. "How are you?"

"I—I'm thirsty."

"Have they hurt you?"

"I don't know what you mean," Ethel said. Her pupils were pin-points.

"Your father sends his love."

"Oh, does he?" She could not have been more uninterested, she looked at Ballas. "I'm thirsty. Please can I have some water?"

Ballas said to Mannering: "Are you satisfied?"

"I'd like her to hear what we say."

"If it makes any difference," Ballas said. "She was—obstreperous." He used the word very carefully. "We had to keep her under sedation." He motioned her away, and obediently she went to one side and sat down on a tapestry-covered carved stool. Cyrus Lake gave her some water from a vacuum jug close to Ballas's hand.

"You had to keep Ricardi quiet, too," Mannering remarked when she was settled.

Ballas's lids drooped over his eyes again, and Mannering had the feeling that he was in physical pain. It was a long time before he said :

"Yes. I'm afraid that was what upset Ethel. But it *is* possible to start something you can't stop."

"When you can't stop what you've started, you're losing your grip."

"Yes," admitted Ballas slowly. "I guess you're right. A man can get old and tired. But I want to tell you something. *You* are as responsible as I for what happened to Ricardi."

"Because I escaped from here?"

"Because you escaped." Ballas repeated the words heavily. "Oh, I am not blaming you, but facts are facts."

"Here's a fact," Mannering said. "Let Ethel Alundo go, and I'll do a deal with you over the film."

"What kind of deal?"

"Better than the one you offered."

"I didn't talk of terms," Ballas said flatly.

"You offered all you possessed," Mannering said. "I will settle for less. I will settle for all there is in this room. Everything, under a deed of gift to anyone I name, for services rendered by me. Everything," Mannering repeated, "except the chair you're sitting on, the table in front of you and any one other piece you would like to keep."

"And for all this, you will give me the microfilm?" Ballas asked flatly.

Mannering did not know why he hesitated. To lie would have been so simple; and if ever there was a man to whom to lie would have been forgivable it was Ballas. Yet he did hesitate; and the pause dragged on and on until the moment came when he realised that he had lost his chance to lie.

Had there ever been one?

Mannering had a sense of knowing this old man's mind; in some odd way he felt almost as if there were some strange affinity between them. He himself could divine when some people lied to him and Ballas probably had the same gift. At a lift of his finger, Ballas could set these men on to him, to do exactly what they had done to Ricardi—or worse.

"No," he said. "It's too important to be in the hands of any one individual."

"And you expect me to pay you for—*nothing*?"

"Not for nothing," Mannering said. "For the absolute certainty that this weapon can never be used."

"There can be no certainty."

"If I convince you that there is, will you deal?"

"I cannot be convinced," Ballas said wearily. "Had you never escaped from me, had you never dealt with the F.B.I., had you never attacked my men on the elevated railway— then you might have convinced me. Not now."

"I can try," Mannering said.

"Yes, you may try."

Mannering put his hand to his breast pocket but before he actually touched it, two revolvers were trained on him. He looked at each, shrugging, glanced at Ethel, who seemed to take no notice but was playing with her glass, and took out his wallet. He extracted the locker key he had brought from the hotel and placed it on the desk in front of Ballas.

"That's a locker at the Conrad Hilton Hotel," he said. "The nearest one to the shoe-shine parlour. In it there is a fake film—one which I once thought of trying to pass off to you as the real one."

Ballas put out a hand and touched the key.

"Mario," Cyrus Lake said, "he's everything O'Leary said. Don't let him fool you again."

"Cyrus," said Mannering, "I'm disappointed in you."

"I'm not disappointed in you." Cyrus moved so that he could see Mannering more closely, and the half-amused smile on the well-shaped lips, the gleam in the fine eyes. "You're the best we've come up against in all the thirty years I've worked with Mario Ballas. And if I can prevent it, no one is going to sell him down the river. You've gone nearer than any man we've ever met. Hasn't he, Mario?"

"Yes," Ballas said. "Tell Mannering what you know, Cyrus."

"I've had three reports," Cyrus said. "You've spent time

with the F.B.I. agents you met at the elevated. They drove
you first to the Conrad Hilton, then to the Palmer House
Hotel. The next morning you went back to the Conrad
Hilton—Mannering, there isn't an hotel in Chicago where
we haven't a man. If you thought you could throw us off the
scent by dealing with Tiger and a phoney cowboy suit, you
were wrong."

"So I was wrong," Mannering said. "And what else?"

"You talked to Captain Pollitzer of San Antonio Police
Headquarters."

"What about?"

"That I don't know."

"Perhaps I will tell you," Mannering said. "Is there
more?"

"You've been to see Alundo, and Alundo has a guest
from England. The doorman at Lake View keeps us informed."

"Now *I'm* keeping you informed," Mannering said. "The
man from England is Lord Fentham, Chairman of the Peace
Group Alundo belongs to. They don't trust America not to
use this weapon—nor do they trust Russia. They don't believe that any one country should have it, nor any group of
countries. Alundo is due to make his Peace Lecture at the
HemisFair in San Antonio next week, and he wants to
destroy both copies of the microfilm in front of his audience.
He —"

Ballas's eyes were blazing, his hands were clenching and
unclenching—that tell-tale sign of anger. Once or twice his
lips moved, and at last he could contain himself no longer.

"You're *mad*, Mannering! I've told you the facts about
Alundo."

"He says exactly the same thing about you."

"To hell with what he says! He's in the pay of the Communists, he'll do whatever they tell him to do."

"I don't believe it," Mannering stated flatly. He turned

to Ethel, who was no longer drooping on the stool but sitting upright. The effects of the drug were quickly wearing away, Mannering noticed. "And what do *you* think?" he asked her.

She leaned forward. "I—I don't *know*," she said helplessly. "I've never *liked* his work for peace—I thought he was getting too involved. Then when he telephoned me and asked me to bring the package —" She broke off.

"Did you know what was in it?" Mannering asked quietly.

"Not until after that man attacked us in Ricky's apartment," said Ethel. "Oh, it was all such a *muddle*. I hadn't seen Ricky since he came to England to ask Daddy to speak at the HemisFair—when he burst into your room at the Conrad Hilton and said Daddy had sent him to collect the package, he signalled to me to pretend I didn't know him—oh why did he and Daddy have to make such a *mystery* out of everything! I didn't know *who* to believe, *who* to trust. Ricky told me a little bit about it on the way round to his apartment, but not all—then, as soon as we got there, that man attacked us—he'd already knocked Daddy out—and stole the briefcase. You must have arrived just afterwards. Daddy told me the rest—what the microfilm really was—after you'd gone —"

"And then I persuaded her to come and talk to me about it—I wanted to convince her that I would make better use of the film than her father would," Ballas interpolated. "The film wasn't in the briefcase, and I thought she—or her father—had tricked me. I know now that it was you. *What did you do with that film, Mannering? Where is it now?*" Ballas's voice was low, and by that lowness created a greater sense of urgency, of menace.

Mannering ignored him, turning back to Ethel.

"So you came to see Ballas, thinking that he had the film and hoping that you might be able to get it back from him.

And so that your father would not be too disappointed if you failed you told him that you were going to see me."

Ethel nodded.

"And then you found that Ballas didn't have it after all—and that he intended to keep you prisoner, hoping to get the film in exchange for your safety. And Ricardi guessed what had happened and tried to rescue you."

"Mannering," Ballas interpolated, "Ricardi used to work for me—that's how he knew how anxious I was to get Alundo's copy of the film. But he changed sides and started to help Alundo. Instead of giving *me* information, he kept it back and lied to me. Don't blame Ethel for what happened to Ricardi—it didn't happen because he came to rescue her."

Almost wearily, Mannering said : "No, I won't blame Ethel for that or anything. Not even for telling the police I was on the Broadway Limited when Enrico was killed. You did do that, didn't you Ethel?"

"I told Mario," she answered.

"And I told the police," Ballas finished. He sounded very tired. "I knew a lot about you, Mannering, and I didn't want the added risk of tangling with you. I had plenty to do already. Oh, I knew *you* hadn't murdered Enrico—but it suited me, for a time at least, to pretend that I thought you had."

"Do you know who *did* murder your nephew?"

Slowly, steadily, Mario Ballas looked at each man in the room. Did his gaze linger a little longer on Tiger O'Leary, Mannering wondered. Then he leaned back.

"Mannering, I've finished talking. Either you give me the film or tell me how to get it, or I shall have to make you talk. I don't want to," he went on bleakly. "But if I must, believe me I won't fail."

Mannering said very quietly: "We'll have to find that out. But before we do, there are one or two things you ought to know. When I came here I had a miniature tape recorder in my pocket. It was taken away. Where is it?"

"I've got it," Cyrus Lake put in.

"Play it, will you?" Mannering said. "If you can't operate it, I will."

"I can operate it."

"Cyrus," Ballas said, "he's the kind of madman who would blow himself up so as to blow us up."

"I've checked it for explosive, Mario."

"It could be a booby trap which goes off while it's being played."

"I ran a spare tape through it," Cyrus said.

"Play it," ordered Ballas.

Cyrus plugged the little machine into a point near the desk, and Mannering sat back. The three men there to watch him stood impassively : they were morons, this scene, or probably any other, meant nothing to them. O'Leary coughed occasionally, the sound a short bark of protest. Ballas kept his eyes closed, but his tension showed in his expression, in the way he clenched his hands on the desk.

First came Mannering's voice, then Alundo's; next Alundo's in anger, then Alundo telling Mannering exactly what he would do at the HemisFair, calling Ballas evil incarnate, speaking with a controlled passion which seemed to be more effective as it came out of the box—detached from the anger and the wildness in Alundo's eyes. For the first time the faint smile was wiped from Cyrus Lake's face, and something of the tension touched him, too.

At last, Alundo's voice and Mannering's faded.

CHAPTER TWENTY

The Speech

MANNERING leaned forward and switched the recorder off, then sat back and waited. Cyrus began to walk about, dabbing at the back of his neck with a very white handkerchief. Ballas sat hunched in his chair. Ethel was standing very erect, still holding her glass; she had listened, fascinated, as her father's voice had come into the room.

"And you believe, if he gets it back, he will destroy the microfilm?" Ballas asked slowly.

"Yes," said Mannering, "I do believe it. I don't think you are right about Alundo. I think he's an idealist who believes he can save the peace of the world in this way. And I think he should have a chance to try."

Ballas shrugged.

"And I don't believe he will endanger that peace," Mannering added. "After all, you do know that *that* wasn't a sell-out to the Russians—or to anyone else."

Ballas was brooding.

"Mario," Cyrus said. "Mannering could still be lying to you."

"He's not lying," said Ballas, with quiet certainty. "He's keeping plenty back, but he's not lying. Tell me what happens if I refuse the deal, Mannering."

"You will be raided."

"Where?"

"Here."

"The Mexican police will never come here for me."

"They'll come for me," Mannering said simply.

Ballas said softly : "So."

"They'll come for me," Mannering repeated, "and they will come into this room. I have told them how to. I've told them if needs be they can blow a hole through the roof. It would be sacrilege, but — What do you think of Pollitzer?" he added almost casually.

Nothing could keep the smile away from Cyrus Lake's lips for long.

Ballas said without feeling : "He is a dedicated man."

"Dedicated to putting you in prison."

"There is nothing he would like more."

"*Pollitzer* might do it," Cyrus Lake breathed.

"Pollitzer will send Mexican police here if I am not out with Ethel at the stroke of seven o'clock," Mannering said. "I made a deal with him, too. If Ethel and I get out, he won't contact the Mexican police. And you can enjoy your treasures for as long as —"

"I live," Ballas interrupted, dryly. "To whom would you want me to leave them, Mannering?"

Mannering said quietly: "The one thing Alundo has always wanted is a World Peace Foundation with some teeth in it. These"—he spread his arms—"must be worth twenty or twenty-five million dollars. Endow a Peace Foundation. If *you* haven't lied to *me*," Mannering went on softly, "that is basically what *you* want."

"*I* believe in America," Ballas said thinly.

"America needs peace as much as anyone," Mannering replied. He smiled at Cyrus Lake. "You could give your name to the foundation—yours, and Alundo's. Your memory would really be revered then, instead of —"

"I don't need telling how I shall be regarded after my death," Ballas interrupted. "Can you guarantee that Alundo will behave as you think he will?"

"No."

"Mario," Cyrus said, "look at this straight. You don't

stand to gain a thing. Not a damned thing. You give all, you take nothing. Mannering's putting over a big confidence trick—my God, Yellow Kid Wiel never thought up one as big as this. Give me everything you've got, he says, and I won't give you anything in return."

Cyrus dabbed at his neck.

Mannering said : "You have about ten minutes to make up your mind. If I walk out of this house and radio San Antonio within ten minutes, you can live in peace for the rest of your life, enjoy living, and even get a lot of fun out of the fact that you're a kind of partner to Alundo —"

Ballas laughed, a strange, not entirely unamused, thread of sound.

Mannering thought with growing excitement: It's come off. He's going to do it. My God, he's going to do it! A surge of relief, of humble triumph, touched him.

He was rejoicing, his heart lighter than he had known it for a long, long time, when there came a sharp buzz of sound. It went through him like an electric shock. O'Leary leaned forward and flicked down a switch.

"What is it? *What!*" He turned to the others excitedly. "The police are at the front door! What do we do—keep them out or let them in?"

Mannering thought with awful disappointment : They're early, they're too early.

Ballas said: "So they *are* outside." He pressed a button, and the door release clicked and buzzed, as he said to Mannering : "You had to lie. You had to say they were coming at —"

Before he finished, before Mannering could begin to think, O'Leary swung round, revolver in hand, rage in his eyes, malevolence on his bruised face. He levelled the gun at Mannering, and said :

"You aren't going to live to see them."

And he fired.

Mannering flung himself to one side.

He was aware of the awful danger, of looking into the face of death. He felt the sickening impact of the bullet in his left arm, level with his heart. He went staggering sideways, off his balance, fear greater than pain. He heard the sound of more shooting, but felt no further impact. He came up against a stool and went sprawling, the room going round and round, the only sound now the blur of voices. Then a girl's face hovered above his and he felt hands touching him gently.

"Are you all right? Please, *please*, are you all right?"

Someone said : "He's dead."

"No," said Mannering, "I'm not dead."

The girl said: "It's his arm. I think it's only his arm."

"I—am—not—dead."

Another face appeared, familiar, but no longer smiling. Cyrus Lake's.

"O'Leary is dead," he said. "You're okay." He turned round. "He's okay, Mario. It's just his arm."

The arm was aching only a little, the main sensation was of numbness. Now, questions crowded into Mannering's mind, one of them of overwhelming importance.

"What about the police?"

Ethel was saying: "Scissors, we want some scissors, to cut the sleeve off. Oh, and water and towels."

"No cops," Cyrus said.

"But O'Leary —"

"O'Leary lied," Cyrus said. "He wanted an excuse to get even with you for beating him up. Even more important, he wanted to convince Mario that it really *was* you, and not he, who had killed Enrico—and thought it would be easier to do this if you weren't around to defend yourself. Mario soon discovered that it was O'Leary who had done the killing—but like he said, it suited his books to pretend he thought you'd done it. As soon as O'Leary realised that Mario *didn't* believe it was you who murdered his nephew, he was afraid suspicion might fall on him and knew he had to act quickly."

"But how —"

"One of the guards got on the house phone to ask if he and another couple of guards should relieve that trio." Cyrus nodded towards the three men who had been brought in to watch Mannering and who were still standing there, impassive as ever. "O'Leary took the call and then told us the man had rung through to warn us that the police had arrived. There are no cops here yet—not outside the front door, anyway. There are plenty out in the mesa, pretending to hide. Do you think you can go and talk to them before they come?"

"Yes," Mannering said.

Ethel was cutting away the sleeve of his jacket.

"That is if Mario —" Mannering began.

Cyrus said: "Mario, he wants to hear you say it."

Mario Ballas came slowly across the room. He was smiling, tight-lipped. He carried a sealed packet, a big yellow envelope, in his hand. He sat on a stool which one of the others pushed into position, and looked down at Mannering.

"I will do what you want," he said, and held out the packet. "Here is my copy of the microfilm, concealed in the Fentham jewels." He put it into Mannering's free hand, and for a moment each of them held it; then Ballas let go. "You had better be right," he added, almost bitterly. "You had better be right."

"Why don't you come to the HemisFair, and hear for yourself?" asked Mannering.

Arm strapped to his side, Mannering stepped out of the

house and walked across the courtyard. As he did so, Captain Pollitzer and a Mexican police officer walked from the corner, solid, unafraid. Mannering raised the envelope, and Pollitzer raised his left hand. Ethel came down the steps hesitantly. Mannering waited for her.

"Some things we keep to ourselves," he murmured.

"Am I glad to see you two," Pollitzer said loudly, advancing. "What's happened to your arm?"

"Ballas had to repress a revolt," Mannering answered. "But it's all right, it's all over. Could I go into details later? This damned arm —"

His arm did not prevent him from talking as a police pilot flew them back to San Antonio.

Within an hour he was in hospital, by morning he was ready to go out again, rested, bandaged, more contented than he had been for a long time. Ethel was on her way to Chicago; Fentham and Professor Alundo had been told of the recovery of both copies of the microfilm. Mannering, not sure whether to go back to England or whether to sun himself in Texas, heard a forthright voice—Steven Marshall's—just outside his door.

The door opened.

"Good morning, John," Marshall said briskly. "I want you to know I'm proud to know you."

"Oh, nonsense," disseminated Mannering.

"It's not nonsense," Marshall declared. "My wife and I hope you'll stay with us from now through the opening day and Professor Alundo's lecture. That lecture is a sell-out already." He stood squarely in front of Mannering. "And Patsy and I hope you will call your wife in London and ask her to come and visit us, also. You surely will be welcome."

"You'll love them," Mannering said to Lorna. "And they really mean it when they say they'll be happy to see you."

"We most certainly will," said Patsy Marshall, who was sitting opposite him in the house in San Antonio—a house modelled almost on La Racienda. She was small, dark, alert, eager.

Lorna's voice sounded faint, but clear, at the other end of the line.

"If you're sure," she said, "I'd love to come over."

Mannering nodded.

"Why, that's wonderful!" Patsy exclaimed.

Mannering, Lorna, the Marshalls, and the thousands who had laboured to get the HemisFair ready on time, paid homage at last to the great opening day of parades and speeches of welcome, beneath the unfurled flags of all fifty States and nearly as many nations.

They sat in the enormous Convention Centre with Mario Ballas and Cyrus Lake.

There was not a seat to spare in the vast auditorium, but everywhere there was a hum of conversation. It slackened, stopped, then turned into a roar of applause as Steven Marshall walked briskly on to the stage.

He introduced Professor Alundo in thirty-three seconds flat, and led the applause when Alundo appeared. The Professor stood, small, grey, and lonely, on the great stage; but as he began to speak, a confidence, a sincerity, even a grave nobility, radiated from him. The microphones carried his voice clearly, each word articulated with great care as he dealt with the problems of finding world peace, of calming anxious, frightened peoples.

Then, he held up the two microfilms.

He told the breathless audience what they were; and in front of their eyes, he burned them. And while the flames leapt up from a silver plate, his words drifted, sure and unforgettable, to the hearts of the anxious watchers.

". . . and the time will come when swords must be turned

into ploughshares and when the lion shall lie down with the lamb . . ."

Suddenly, those in front of him were cheering. The white and the black and the yellow, men of great nations and men of small, all rose to their feet, and cheered and cheered and cheered again.

Mannering saw the tears in Ethel's eyes.

He saw a strange peace in Mario Ballas's face as the old man looked away from the excited throng, smiled very faintly at Mannering, and held out his hand. On one side of him was Fentham, on the other Cyrus Lake; both noticed this gesture and were glad.

Three days later, the Mannerings arrived at London Airport, and as they passed through Customs, newspapermen and television men descended on them . . .

"John," Lorna said afterwards, "I've never been so proud of you."

"I've never felt so good," Mannering said.

Her glance lightly touched his arm.

"Not really bad," answered Mannering, smiling at her. "Everything considered, we got off very lightly." He was thinking of how close to death he had been and how badly Ricardi had been hurt, yet how well they had all come out of the situation.

Ricardi was recovering; Ethel was at the hospital each day, he was told.

In Chicago, Ballas's attorneys were drawing up the Deed of Foundation.

In Los Angeles Professor Alundo was addressing audiences which gave him a tumultuous welcome, while the television companies were clamouring for interviews.

Fentham, his jewels recovered, was returning to England by sea.

The Mexican police were investigating the death of Tiger O'Leary and the newspapers were crying:

CHICAGO GANGSTER SLAIN

Mannering felt tired; pleasantly and cheerfully tired. It was good to be home, good to have his wife by his side, good to see in the English papers a mood of great optimism in world affairs. There would be setbacks, of course, and new problems; but he had a feeling that nothing would seem quite so bad again.